Marcus Grey

By Don Six

To Grammie K, you taught me that magic exists in this world and that it didn't have to come from a box, even if it sometimes came from a box. Hava Nagila.

First paperback edition April 2021

ISBN: 9798726019437

Book design by Donald Six

Chapter One

"My name is Marcus Grey, and I am a Magic addict."
This had been Marcus' first conscious thought every morning for the last three years and admitting it always made him feel stronger for the day. Marcus woke up as he always did, five minutes before his five o'clock alarm, one leg out of the sheets, hugging a pillow that had made its way out of its case in his sleep. He instinctively flipped the pillow he was lying on to the cool side and let it soothe the impact the day had somehow already caused to his face. The only break from the norm that he could make out from the bed was that the rainstorm that had kicked up the night before had managed to clean some of the dirt off their balcony, the rhythmic drips that had drummed him to sleep had subsided into a soft mist. Just on the other side of the exterior half

wall, he could make out the building across the way. He watched for a minute as the other early risers flicked their lights on, bringing to life the closest thing to a sunrise that the city would see through the thick blanket of clouds that blotted out the sky, reflecting the light back in on itself in a soft orange hum. But, for all the gray that the New York morning promised, today held the potential for a greater light than appearances would suggest. Marcus shifted in the bed, sliding up just far enough to get the leverage he needed to open the bedside table drawer. He reached over and pulled out, as quietly as he could, a small blue velvet ring box.

Wallace rustled next to him. She was not an early riser, but she was a much lighter sleeper than he was. Marcus flicked open the box to give the ring a quick look. He smiled relaxed as he verified for the first time since he checked it the night before that it was still there. In the dark silence he reflected on his plan for the day.

He would start with work as normal. Mike Heinkel, Marcus' boss at the garage, had given him a half day off to prepare, once work was over, he would pick up the last remaining fixings that he needed for the evening meal and take them over to his neighbors for meal prep. Their neighbor, an old man who insisted he be called "Sarge", had agreed to allow Marcus to cook in his apartment in exchange for free apartment sitting and taking care of his birds for a few weeks as he was away. It would have been a fair trade had it not been for the birds.

There were four of those birds. The way that they managed to somehow emotionally scar Marcus every time he watched them left him positive that they were geniuses, even by human standards. He no longer doubted that they premeditated their plans before he came over to feed them. Through a coordinated effort, and military strategy, they usually ended up with two of them escaping into the apartment as another ran interference in some grandiose flight around Sarge's few commemorative military glasses and challenge coins, often risking harm to itself and the collectibles. Inevitably, Marcus would end up injured by a coffee table or a falling object as he was forced to dance around the apartment trying to grab the escaped bird. While all of this happened, the fourth bird, a black raven named Herschal, which would sit on Sarge's chair and watch silently, a lipless smile shining in his black onyx eyes. It was barely worth it but being able to cook in Sarge's apartment worked in Marcus' favor because not having to worry about Wallace coming home early was a great benefit when preparing his specialty, a cranberry and brie chicken with apple chutney, the meal he had made for her on their first date. If she walked in on this special meal, she would undoubtedly figure that something was happening. Which is why today worked perfectly into Marcus' proposal plan. Today marked the three-year mark of Marcus' sobriety if he got caught, he would blame the celebration on that.

Three continuous years of being clean of magic and at Group tonight, Marcus planned to give a speech thanking Wallace for the part that she had played in it. He had been attending Group from three times a week to every day of the week for the past two and a half years, depending on need. While technically the organization was called "Magicians Anonymous", there was a more relaxed group of individuals, most of them regulars, who craved the support that Magicians Anonymous offered but needed something that did not feel so structured. Thus, the Group was born. It runs exactly like Magicians Anonymous, but instead of reporting magic user information back to the government as Magicians Anonymous did per the Federal mandate, Group respected anonymity. So, Group's regulars had become Marcus' closest friends and allies. He was excited to share the day with them. More so, he was excited about starting the rest of his life with Wallace.

At this point, she had been with him for his entire journey, at least the most influential leg. She acted as his light and way, a magical path through the darkness of addiction. She knew everything about him, his good and bad. She knew him better than most of even his closest friends, and unlike many of the voyeurs along the way, she stuck around. They had first met when she became his nurse in rehab and listened to the most honest and raw stories about his life. In her, and through her love, he had found someone who could hear who he was and not turn away, understanding that his past was something that he was looking to turn away from, but in years of downward spirals, had turned himself around enough to not be able to find a way out. She spent all the time that she had helping to show him that path.

The first day he was out of the program he contacted her on the number she had given him and asked her out. It hadn't been a match made in heaven and at best of times it barely made it in the real world, but they had made it work. Communication, dedication, trust got them through every slump and every fight since they had moved in 8 months after meeting. It had been its own kind of perfect.

He smiled and felt her shuffle behind him quickly placing the box back in the drawer and then tried sliding it shut as slowly and quietly as possible. Marcus jolted as a sudden freezing stab ran through his back causing him to slam the drawer shut making more noise than he had intended.

Wallace let out a conquering laugh. She had put her freezing feet on his back and used the leverage to launch herself from lying curled in the bed to wrapping around his body like an overly affectionate orangutan. Poised on top of him for a playful pin, Wallace's bed messed brown pixie-cut hair dangled perfectly down towards him, a mess of playful chaos, and she smiled a grin that he had seen a thousand times. It scrunched her green eyes and drew long laugh lines down her face that framed her freckles and drew a map of love on her flushed chipmunk cheeks.

"Kiss of DEATH!" she hissed, hurling her head forward for a morning breath laced kiss. Marcus faked left and rolled right under her. At over a foot taller than Wallace and much stronger, it didn't take much effort for him to gain the advantage.

"You cannot kill what has already consumed death!" he yelled back, feigning a demonic voice, closing out the kiss. They giggled like teenagers, reminiscent of young love, and pushed each other back to their spots in the bed.

Wallace crawled back over him, kissing him on the cheek, "Whatcha' got in there?" She reached playfully over towards the nightstand Marcus had failed to close entirely.

"Nothing!" He jumped, pushing the drawer shut the remainder of the way, angling his body and reaching back to contain her.

She gave him a look, one that he knew too well. It came naturally for a nurse who had been watching addicts' relapse cycle for years to look at an addict and see the potential for deceit, especially when they were clearly hiding something. It wasn't that she expected of him, as she had reassured him so many times before, it was, as she insisted, just a habitual look of suspicion. But for obvious reasons she thought that he was hiding something, he knew she knew he was hiding something. He scrambled for the best excuse.

"It's... uhm... just my speech for tonight," he lied, "it's... it isn't done yet. I don't want you to see it until it's perfect." It passed without question as she rolled away and picked up her phone and she started making her way through whatever news feeds had the most notifications. Marcus unclenched as he saw any hint of investigative interest disappeared from her aura, her focus now in the other lives that had updated overnight. He left the bed and kicked off the morning routine.

He was always first, he was normally up first, and his routine was shorter. This was mostly, he joked, because in the right side of his shoulder length brown hair, he had a scarred spot, that was, unquestionably, the shape and sized of a clothing iron, and turned the upper half of his ear into a reflective, fleshy cauliflower that partially molded both together and that was attached to the side of his head around the top peak of the ear. Not having to clean behind both ears was what gave him the time advantage. This was what he considered to be the only gift that his father had ever given him from his childhood. His father hadn't even given Marcus the opportunity to find the strength to leave, he went off and died in a train accident. Body burnt to a crisp. No remains. No closure. Decades of abuse, left open to

9

echo through Marcus in the few quiet moments of his life.

But even the harsh reminder of a distant childhood in the dim light of morning had become an opportunity to laugh with Wallace's help. He looked at his face, his blue eyes a little sunken, and his skin was worn but healthy looking with that glow that people in recovery often have. Marcus had the perpetual look of being tired and just a bit dirty, dark dry areas of skin patchworking his body. This was one of the effects of the Drain, the magical force that demanded its own cost for casting. Most addicts who had been casting for as long as he had showed much worse wear from the Drain, but that's because most addicts like Marcus were dead.

Spell casting was all well and good and, in reality, a reasonably sized minority of people had tried casting once or twice. Ever since the Nine Fonts, mysterious magical epicenters that had released the use of magic, had been discovered a few decades before Marcus was born, there weren't many people who could say they hadn't tempted at least once, even just to do something as simple as find their missing keys. The only thing that ever stopped those who were interested was the Drain.

Casters could cast a spell to do something like move a chair and in return for pulling out the chair, their muscles would be sore as if they had moved ten chairs. But you could work at it, making these effects from the Drain less and less, until moving a chair was more like moving a chair, or even less effort than that. This was where hardcore addicts, like Marcus, started to experience issues.

Magic allowed you to build a natural immunity to the negative side effects, in turn allowing stronger spells to be cast, returning to a cycle of more dangerous effects. Spells are smart, and, like a virus, they do their best to keep their host alive. So, in cases where a spell starts to demand too much energy, the spell starts sacrificing non-essential function first. Fingernails, teeth, and hair all fall out first. Your skin gets dry and flakes. Speech gets slurred and vision becomes blurry if you keep it at all. This was the Drain and it would always win out in the end, killing the host, but for a few like Marcus, it was worth it to run the risk.

With magic, you could do anything, and with that there became a collection classification of magic types and users, as established by all governments around the world which were used primarily for ways to identify and criminalize magic use. Marcus was, during the time that he was casting, was what was considered the middle of the road caster, something the government had called Street Addicts. These were the most common addicts, often people who either didn't have jobs or bounced from job to jobs and had the same luck with housing. There were worse addicts who would lose track of reality and better addicts who seemed to have functioning lives but in the end, they were all addicts and among the discards of society, and among them Marcus was pretty average.

That is, except for the classification of his magic type. During the time that he was actively casting, Marcus became something that most addicts feared becoming, he was a Destructive. Destructives were just like any other casters, but they destroyed things, casting from a place of rage and hate, creating destruction that often becomes something unmanageable. On quite a few occasions that had landed Marcus in jail but for the money he could make as a caster it was worth it or, at least in Marcus' case, it used to be worth it. For a couple thousand dollars he would be hired by people who needed a house demolished and didn't want to pay contractors, or someone who didn't want there to be evidence that they were there. He had been part of more than a few insurance scams, racketeering scams, and even a few block clearing efforts by real estate moguls who wanted a certain element driven from their homes. But he had turned his back on that, now he was living for something, or rather, someone.

He grabbed a pair of jeans and a shirt off the floor and, after giving them mostly passing grade on a smell test, pulled them on. In the mirror he looked behind him to the bed, checking to make sure that there hadn't been any movement from Wallace, at least not towards the nightstand.

"How's it goin' hun?" he yelled.

"Peachy keen, babe. Ren says I can take the day off. She is giving one of the new nurses a Hell Week."

Hell Week was the week that Wallace's boss, Ren Darrant, would have the experienced nurses take off on a paid week long break to force the newest nurses through a week of having to figure things out for themselves. Dorian's Cross was the kind of rehab where most patients knew about the Hell Weeks and even helped the nurses gimp along. It wasn't most of their first times through and not likely to be their last, so it benefited them to make friends with the nurses who they saw making it through Ren's grueling process. Dorian's Cross was the location that New York City judges would send repeat offenders of magic abuse and had become the best funded and most practiced rehabilitation facility in the city.

Despite being the kind of venue with repeat customers, Dorian's Cross was a place where patients knew they were there to get better. There wasn't a heart that could stay cold at Dorian's. The nurses really cared, Ren made sure of that, and it made a difference.

Marcus had known Ren before Wallace did. He had witnessed Ren rise from being a nurse, to head nurse, to hospital administrator in a meteoric ascension that had not only forced out an enormous amount of corruption from the hospital administration, but also made Dorian's what it is today. The last time that Marcus was in rehab, Ren had just taken over as Hospital Administrator and was running Hell Week as a pilot program. This was before all of the nurses received compassion training, as well as defensive classes. The nurses were all very new as Ren had forced out any of the nurses who had just been there collecting a check.

Wallace was in the first wave to go through the program. Having only a few skilled nurses, Wallace didn't really have a guiding class that stepped away for her to fill in gaps, there were only gaps. Wallace not only paved the way for the program, but she also created the ideal training documentation and courses for nurses focused on patient relations in making sure that patients were always seen as human first. She was fresh out of Nursing School and her eyes were full of idealistic world changing splendor.

Her knowledge was impressive but, when pitted against the unnerving qualities of true addicts, it was no shield and seeing her struggle in that first week and the time after until she flourished into one of the leading talents at Dorian's was what made Marcus fall in love with her. They grew close through it as he gave her pointers for dealing with some of the patients. He had a lot of first hand experience with The Drain and knew how to talk to people who were experiencing some of its many potential psychotic effects. She was like a student of his more than a patient of hers and she saw him as more than a patient, but as a mentor and friend. Six years of regular trips to rehab for one reason or another really had left him a professional in dealing with patients with varying degrees of the more lasting effects of The Drain. Three years later she was too.

"You deserve the time," he said, then it hit him that he would then need to sneak everything that he had in the apartment next and her being home was a new wrench. "Gonna spend it here?"

"Nah, Stace is looking to hang out today, I'll just meet you at Group tonight?"

It was perfect, "Of course! Have a fun one!" He would have to be stealth, but at least there was a better chance that she wouldn't be around. Once her coworker and best friend, Stacy, had her hooks in her, Wallace would be out all day. Stacy had that effect. She was the kind of person who would be over for a cup of coffee that somehow turned into an overnight party that then became a weekend of pillow forts and karaoke. It wasn't that she wasn't a ton of fun, she was, but Wallace's friends were all tornadoes of seizing life and they were often seizing Marcus' life. Life that could be otherwise spent resting after working all week or going for runs like Wallace wanted. Marcus shook his head of the thoughts of how Stacy could derail his plans and counted his blessings. Once she was out, Wallace would be out all day. That was the Stacy Way.

With a quick kiss and a "Later, hun!" he grabbed the ring and speech from his drawer and Wallace took over the bathroom. He made his way out the door, down the four floor walk up, and onto the wet stone stairs of the entrance leading down to the sidewalk, a sea of monochrome masses sliding across the surface on their way to work.

The rain itself had slowed enough for a New Yorker to be more inconvenienced by having to carry an umbrella for the rest of the day, so he slipped into the stream of commuters, shuffling along with them as he thumbed the ring box, envisioning her face, envisioning the future that he had always pictured. The house in the suburbs, the kids, the...

As he stepped off the curb to cross the street down from his building, massive wrenching force pulled him back off his feet and he stumbled backwards spinning into a crowd of people. Standing in front of him, holding his shoulder, was a five foot tall, black spiked hair, smiling woman, her teeth gleaming white in the dull morning, her sharp canines rivaling those of a TV vampire.

"Whoa there, golden boy." As she grinned at him a taxi flew past the waiting crowd, the driver screaming at Marcus to do something that, while he did not speak the language the taxi driver was screaming, he was sure was akin to "Look out, bud!" with a few indigenous and creative expletives. The short woman coughed refocusing Marcus' attention.

"Thanks." Marcus simultaneously nodded his appreciation and shrugged her hand off his shoulder, the light had changed to walk and her grip had grown to hurt a little. He headed off.

"I'll see you later, Golden Boy!" He would have heard her call after him had he actually been listening, but he was already back to thinking about the ring. He forgot her with the same ease that she disappeared into the crowd.

Work at the garage started and everyone saw that he was distracted with his excitement, regularly stopping in the middle of a job to talk about his plans. He got put on menial tasks, tire rotations and oil changes, and everyone supported him.

Marcus was good in the shop and had been a mentor to many of the guys who were just starting out on exotic vehicle maintenance and restoration, but in three years of 10 hour days, missing one day in the entire time for his father's funeral, he was good.

Sal's Garage had been good to him, and the owner, Richie Behnkowitz, had been even better. Rich was a 86 year old mechanic who could hear a car and tell you the part number of the part that was broken and which of the screws needed to be tightened. Rich had done everything that he could to give as much of his knowledge as he could to Marcus.

Marcus had joined Richie as part of a transitional program meant to take recovering addicts and give them a source of income. In many cases it would lead to a reliable enough source that most addicts would then be able to purchase whatever components that they needed for whatever addiction they wanted to jump back into. But for people like Marcus, who knew Sal's was a good gig as soon as Richie had shook their hand, it was a chance to be a better person. Richie was the kind of person who did good in everything that he could and believed that others could too.

The good radiated from Richie, who was a tough old Israeli Jew with tattoos that had faded so much he claimed he worried that he would be allowed to be buried next to his ex-wife who was, herself, buried in a Jewish cemetery. He had gotten the tattoos when they divorced over thirty years ago and they faded in ways that the betrayal from the love of his life abandoning him hadn't. She was a consistent joke of his in the shop, along with the everlasting love of marriage, but today he kept even those jokes to himself, letting a man in love be a man in love.

After about four hours into the day, Richie pulled the guys off their projects and had bought a few pies from the pizza joint around the corner. He didn't say any sort of congratulations, but he did tell Marcus to go home and have some extra time, letting Marcus know that he would consider it free paid time off if he would also like tomorrow off as well. Marcus was more than thankful as he accepted the offer along with a few fist bumps and high fives on his way out. They were a good team. Marcus smiled as he reentered the cold dreariness of the wet winter day, bleeding a little color into the gray.

It didn't take long for him to run to the market to grab some fresh brie. His conversation with Raju, who was running the market as his father was out, was short and quick, nothing but a nod and a "How's it goin'?".

Marcus was a man with a mission. His legs carried him, dodging through traffic, back to the apartment building, his excitement carried him up the stairs past the ever-growing graffiti and work wanted postings. Marcus opened Sarge's apartment door and dropped off the ingredients he had picked up.

Sarge's apartment looked like it belonged to an old guy named "Sarge". A once nice leather recliner hunched alone, its tattered parts revealing secret favorite places, and one wooden chair at an old wooden table with a book in the center. The times Marcus had been in here it had either been political or from a middle shelf spy thriller. His bed had perfect hospital corners and you could bounce a quarter off the comforter.

The only sign of connection in Sarge's life was his birds. They were also the only source of color that wasn't a simple earth-tone. He had three little tropical birds, parakeets if the food bag were to be any indication, but Marcus knew them better than that. Marcus knew them by name. Somehow that gave them power.

Toko, Renard, Molly, and Herschal. The four birds of the apocalypse.

Their cage took up nearly half the back of the living room and blocked access to one of the best windows in the place. Herschal, the Raven, had been granted outside the cage privileges by Sarge because the other three seemed to try to add too much energy into his personal space and Sarge was certain that Herschal would kill one of the others if he was sure he could get away with it. Marcus agreed.

Toko, Renard, and Molly were green, orange, and blue respectively and they wouldn't shut up. From the moment that Marcus walked walk into the room they would start their chattering, convinced he was there to serve them, the birds would gather at the entryway door to their enclosure and start flapping at the latches, only settling down as Marcus went to grab their food, only to then have one of them escape through a hatch that had been suspiciously unlocked before Marcus could even get to them.

But today Marcus knew what was coming so he made sure all the latches were secure, that he had had pushed Herschal to the other side of the room so that he wouldn't be able to stir up a distraction and, as if they understood the gravity of the situation, stayed back as food was being swapped out, trays were cleaned, and water was refreshed. They were spoiled by Sarge, but from the looks of things, the occasional interactions that he must have in the hallways and his birds were the only contact he had with the world. Marcus made a mental note that he would have to make sure that he asked him for his life's story next time he saw him, and do his best to draw a more personal connection.

He switched gears, pressing his ear against the wall. They weren't that thin and provided decent privacy, but Marcus hoped that if there was any sign that Wallace was home he would hear it. He couldn't hear anything so he slid out through Sarge's door and over to his, looking for any movement in the hallways, then checking under the door for movement. With an ear against the door he felt pretty comfortable he wouldn't have to lie about his reason for being home early.

As quietly as he had slipped into his apartment, he slipped back out with the rest of the ingredients just in case she was in the hall. He jumped between the two apartments, cleaning his own and preparing food in the other. After a few loops, he was feeling ready for his food to go in the oven, he checked the time. It would be another three hours before he planned to meet Wallace for Group and another hour after that they would be on their way home to eat, so in the fridge the food went and into the apartment he went. With some time to relax on the couch and put on some TV, maybe he would even change into something nice.

The norm at Group was super casual, many people were not as fortunate as Marcus was to have such great support at home and a strong work life, often failing at avoiding relapse and having to start their conversations at Group with "It's been a hard couple of days…" Addiction made life easier, made emotions easier. It was nice to have someone to help share the load. After flipping through the channels and picking a rerun of a childhood cartoon, he walked into the bedroom and started looking through whatever shirts he might have that would go well with jeans, or maybe even the pair of khakis that Wallace forced him to buy so he could look nice when they needed to. But it was wet outside and he really didn't want to wear them, so he settled on a blue shirt.

After pushing aside the remainder of his clothes that were now scattered on the closet floor, he found a box of candles. They had some floral scent that he thought was nice so he took a few out. Because of the factors of his addiction as well as contributing memories that had been factors to him prone to relapse, they had decided to not have candles in the house, but Marcus was ready for the fire to hold a new memory. It would be something that would make him smile instead of something to remind him of his dad. The cigarette burns peppering his body were enough to do that. For a moment he could feel the heat run through him. He closed his eyes and pushed out the sounds of drunken laughter, pushing it out left a void that echoed with the absence of his mother's objections. He felt his body cool and his mind soothe. The candle in his hands now had imprints in them from his fingers forcing their way into the wax.

He grabbed a few others and split his focus between staging the apartment and cartoons. Occasionally he would turn off all the lights, draw the blinds, and click off the cartoons to try and get a good visual of how coming into the apartment would look. Then he would rearrange a few things, turn the lights back on after realizing it was too difficult to arrange in the dark, and then start the lights off to on cycle again. He was in the bedroom fumbling through the dark trying to figure out how many candles were too many candles and was fitting the ring on a candle when he heard a sound, it sounded like jingling. He looked over at the glasses on the table, they weren't moving, outside on the balcony everything looked normal... *Idiot, keys!*

With the ring on a candle in his hand he ran into the living room but was too slow to hide himself from the door as the jingling set with a click and the door burst open, but not who he expected. A tall male form backed into the dark room followed by giggles and a leg that kicked the door shut. Marcus wasn't able to place them but it seemed as though this couple had stumbled into the wrong apartment, he must have not set the lock. He stepped up and out of the shadow that he had been standing in and the mess of limbs that were trying to absorb each other paused as the source of the giggles stopped. A blinding light flashed on.

"Marcus, what are you doing home?" It was Wallace, her eyes wide with shock, her hand still on the light switch.

The man turned around, he was a tall, bald man, generally good looking but for a terribly hooked nose. His eyebrows were thick and raised, revealing green gold eyes and an air of feigned surprise. Marcus could easily push past the man's looks, in fact they barely registered, mostly because he couldn't see it, all he could see was the smeared lipstick on his face. Marcus' face grew hot as his eyes started to water.

"It isn't what it looks like!" Wallace yelled, but the lipstick smears that cloudily framed a growing sneer of pearly straight whites said it was exactly what he thought it was.

Then a sob fell out of Marcus and the tall man let out a snicker. Wallace started to push past the stranger but stopped as she became illuminated by a spark of light that jumped suddenly to the candle in Marcus' hand, igniting the wick, casting frantic shadows in the room that all began searching for a place to hide. She stopped, her stare of concern turning to a gape of horror.

"Marcus..." She paused, shifting her stance from rushing arms-wide to comfort into a defensive one with her hands outstretched as if to block an oncoming blow from hitting her face. "You don't want to do this, think about all you've worked for! All you have..."

In little less than a whisper and with the last of the strength he would be able to muster for the day, he shook his head, "You were what I was working for. You were what I

22

had..." The candle had nearly burnt all the way down to his hand, wax running down his hand in a steady stream. The light of the candle itself turning into a blaze that rivaled a fuel tanker explosion.

"Sweetheart, I..." she couldn't get anything else out before the flame fell from the candle and ran across his sleeve, quickly engulfing his shirt in fire. He reached out, the ring glowing in his hand, he saw it reflecting his body which was glowing as the flame wrapped around his head and ran down his legs.

Wallace pleaded for him to stop but it was too late. Marcus had relapsed.

Chapter Two

Marcus burned white, it was something that he had always liked, not in some sort of a purist kind of way, that would be stupid. He liked that as his body burned he could always see the searing white pain that he had always kept inside of him now prominently displayed on the outside. It was probably why his default response when he was a user was destruction magic. The heat around him felt like home. It felt safe or at least familiar.

He wouldn't feel any pain, he was so familiar with the spell that it shaped around him without needing to be constantly controlled. The wick, continuing to be the spell component that he had to use, burned up in his hand and the Drain began looking for a new source. Spells are interesting in that way, they take on lives of their own, a force to be reasoned with but not controlled. It's one of the reasons that destruction magic was so dangerous. All spells required a component that was used as a focus. You could make it rain over a person with a palm full of water or jump across four lanes of traffic while holding a grasshopper. What made destruction magic different was that it destroyed the focus, almost like a sacrifice.

The flames leaped around his body, looking for a focus for the spell, burning small holes in his clothes until they spindled out to the apartment around him and taking their green couch first. That couch had been the first thing her couple's therapist insisted on them getting to compromise on the fact that she didn't like his old couch. The old couch that he had had since he had first moved out of his childhood home, the one on which he had first kissed her and the one he first told her that he loved her on. But his couch wasn't their couch so they had to trade it for a green one that she thought was cute and hip at IKEA where they had spent too many hours lost in a maze of things that they didn't need to try to afford but did anyway because it would be cute and her friends online had one just like it. Next the table, the entertainment system, the coffee tables, the white square shelves, and the Cafe signs, all compromises where his reward was that the fighting stopped. The spell fed off his anger, it saw the greatest sources of his hate and fed on his soul as it happily burnt the world down around him. His mind raced. Who really won in all of this ash falling to the ground around him? Why was a candle holder worth a fight? Worth this? He turned to Wallace for the first time since he cast.

Wallace, who had watched the destruction for as long as she could, had managed to stay out of it, but Marcus hadn't just engulfed himself in flames, but now the apartment and the floor around him were all in an uncontrollable blaze, he had lost control of the spell. This was the same thing that had gotten him arrested the last time, and she knew it. Her fear turned to dread as the clothes on Marcus' back began to catch flame, holes piercing the protective barrier he had around him and licking at his skin. She grabbed her guest by the coat and started pulling towards the hallway.

Marcus had unintentionally managed to block any route to the fire extinguishers and with each spike of rage intensifying the flames around them the opportunity to flee was waning, so she was going for the fire escape in the hallway. As she pulled this new man along, Marcus followed slowly behind, yells from adjacent apartments filled the halls as smoke detectors started going off. She only looked back once making eye contact with Marcus for one last time before opening the door at the end of the hall and running out. The man stood there for a moment, and looked back at Marcus, raised two finger guns, shot them, blew them out and winked as he ducked into the hallway, this time pulling Wallace out with him.

"Pathetic," the man chuckled back as he disappeared into the smoke that was now billowing out of the open door into the hallway, alarms blaring through the building calling for evacuation.

Marcus let out a scream, or tried to, but The Drain was getting to him. His mouth recoiled in pain from the attempted yell as his suddenly dry, chapped lips split into warm slits dripping blood that dried in an instant from the heat in the room. The power the spell had sapped from his body had been enough for several of his fingernails to fall off and he could feel clumps of hair falling out and watched as a few of them fell and burned in the ambient heat. Every spell had a price, a lot had been taken out. The Drain took what it was owed with a vengeance. He fell exhausted to the floor. The spell had been smart enough to put out any flames and cool the exposed concrete before he collapsed, the building burning with him. It was time to die and he surrendered to the realization that death was all he really had ever wanted. A simple, clean escape from the torture of trying to do the right thing. To be free of who he had chosen to be.

It could have been minutes, it could have been seconds, but he felt two arms wrap around him and start dragging him towards the hallway.

"There is no way that you get to die like this Ra'Saram. Not this time."

Marcus cracked his eyes open just enough to see the man who had come in with Wallace carrying him and he felt a surge of energy and writhed out of the man's grip, falling hard to the floor.

"At least not yet. No, this time will have to be more special than that."

Marcus had regained consciousness but didn't have nearly enough energy to open his mouth, which the blood had dried shut anyway from the smoke and flames. It was then that he realized that he, unlike his apartment, was no longer burning. With two more finger guns and a blown kiss, the man winked and left down the hall and out the fire escape, mixing in with the neighbors who were making their way out in an orderly chaos and muttering of the inconvenience of having to avoid being burnt to death had caused.

He felt his lips crack as he gasped to say something, to have a comeback, a question, anything but there was nothing left in him. He started to crawl, coughing and gasping, below the smoke line above him, only able to pull himself a few inches before collapsing in exhaustion. A few feet kicked passed him, probably unable to see him or more likely unwilling to care. He rolled over onto his back and watched as the flames from his door started to lick over into the hallway. He had seen videos of flashovers online and all he hoped was that the heat would take him and end the days agony, but again he was not that lucky.

Four sets of feet ran up to him, blurry hands reaching down into Marcus' vision, grabbing his hands and legs as they pulled him out onto the fire escape. He couldn't make them out, except that they were all wearing vibrantly colored boots. As the smoke shifted into the darkening gray sky above him and fresh air hit his lungs, before Marcus could see the faces of the people carrying him, they too had disappeared into the crowd, leaving him at the top of the stairs.

It took Marcus everything he had in him to get down the stairs to the alley below and, as the fresh air hit him, his mind cleared and his sense of the time returned. Looking around, he could see that the fire department hadn't arrived, and, luckily, neither had The Regulators. The Regulators, like any government agency used for controlling the masses, was severely bound by red tape from being able to actually do any real work effectively. But even though the Regulation Commission, the group that hired and trained The publishing and decided this would give me more control over the future of my book.

Needing a name for my publishing company, I chose one based on a Bible verse my mother often quoted… "Joy comes in the morning". That name encouraged me to look to the end of the process of writing and know what joy I would experience when my book was printed.

I purchased an ISBN number and bar code for the eventual cataloging and sale of my book.

Since I am a former schoolteacher, my book could have no misspelled words or errors in grammar. After endless spell checks and countless proof reads, I was finally ready to publish.

Then in June, we moved, this time to Sturgis, SD. My book was on hold again until my computer service could be restored. In July, I faxed my manuscript to Jonathan Gullery and RJ Communications who did the final preparation for printing. They also designed the cover.

On July 27, 2008, I had "tweaked" my manuscript for the final time. At last! My book was ready for printing.

As I write the final paragraph in these reflections on becoming an author, I am looking forward to the day I hold *Crawl into the Night* in my hands. I am deeply grateful for the encouragement of students, family and friends, and God's blessings, which made the completion of my book a reality. I wish you success as you follow your own dreams.

I would be happy to hear from you. You may contact me at 1820 Meadow Lark Road, Sturgis, SD 57785 or garyladue@knology.net

Joy comes in the morning!

Regulators, restricted their use of magic and anti-magical abilities, on more than one occasion, these casting police had caught Marcus and were very good at their jobs.

The Regulators not being there yet meant that only a few minutes could have passed since his casting was reported, they were known for sub-ten minute response times. He looked around, scanning the crowd for Wallace but she was not one of the scared and aggravated faces. Sirens wailed in the distance, Fire was on its way and The Regulators would not be far behind. If they saw him, they knew him. Every magic addict repeat offender was known to The Regulators and, while the magic that the government had granted them to use was minimal, their memory enchantments that enhanced their recall abilities made sure that they could spot a known caster at one-hundred yards in a crowd with relative certainty. So Marcus did the only thing he was prepared to do, he ran.

In his singed clothes and with smoke in his lungs he coughed, tasting iron in his mouth. He ran his tongue around his teeth just to make sure and felt them all there, they were. A little blood in his mouth would be expected from the wear of The Drain as the spell had only initially protected him from smoke inhalation. When The Drain kicked in, it would most often target areas that were protected in the spell, getting the cosmic damage it was owed. He spat a bit of blood onto the ground and kicked some dirt over it, knowing that his blood could be used for a tracking spell, and started a brisk walk away from the crowd. A few blocks away he found a cafe to duck into. It was then, blood on his lips, shirt mostly gone, and pants that were more holes than fabric, surrounded by people wrapped in jackets staring at him, that he realized the next worst part of the whole day. He had left his wallet in the apartment.

"For the love of..." He yelled, grabbing his head and collapsing into a booth.

It was unlikely that this was the strangest thing that the people in this New York coffee shop had seen today, and they went back to their drinks after sharing concerned looks with one another, stealing nervous glances at the half naked screaming man who had settled into the booth closest to the door.

A blonde barista, probably in her twenties and by the looks of her she was in the city chasing a dream, maybe of being a model, slid up to his booth, "What can I get for you, sir."

"Just water for now, thanks." Marcus did his best to force a smile and went back to his thoughts.

"Sir, if you're going to sit here, you're going to have to order something."

"I ordered water, how's abouts we start there and see how I feel after seeing the menu." He gave her a smirk and nod that he hoped made his words sound like, "Give me a freaking break here." but he was pretty sure it sounded more like "I'm a danger to everyone here, it's time to panic." He couldn't blame her for the sudden look of fear in her eyes, but he didn't have the time nor the desire to smooth things over.

"Sir, the problem is that we have paying customers who need that seat and," she gestured to a sign at the door, "we do ask that you wait to be seated." Her face shifted to one of a mother negotiating with a child, "I was trying to be fair and let you order, but if you aren't going to purchase food, I'm going to have to ask you to leave." She crossed her arms and popped her hip in victory.

Marcus rolled his eyes and muttered, "Like freaking Area 51 here," going through the motions of patting himself down for his wallet as if it might somehow be resting on his shirt somewhere.

"So can I get you something," the girl asked.

"Can I just have a second, it has been a real day?"

"I'm sorry, sir. If you are going to be in..."

"I know... I have to get something." he interrupted. "I seem to have lost my wallet."

"Then I am sorry, sir. I'm going to have to ask you to leave." She smiled a grin that asserted dominance in a way that Marcus was a bit raw too at this point in his personal Hell to handle appropriately.

Marcus leaned towards her, teeth bared in a smile outlined in ash,soot, and blood and saw her eyes widen. As he pushed himself up from the booth to give her the lashing of a lifetime. The rage he felt was replaced with a shot of excruciating pain in his right hand and he grimaced and fell back into his booth. Dizzying lights entered his vision and danced to the beat of sudden nausea that was threatened to expel the pizza from earlier. In his hand, he saw the ring that he was holding on the candle, it had melted in the flames and seared its way into his flesh. He ran his fingers around it and found the gold fused into his palm, unmoving, the wound around it very much inflamed with infection. One more thing to have to deal with.

When he looked up the waitress was gone and had moved behind the counter, on the phone with someone speaking quickly and pointing her manager, a particularly overweight man Italian man, over to him. Marcus took his cue and bolted out the door before the manager, or the police who were likely on the other end of the phone, could get to him.

As the initial shock of the Drain wore off, his sense of smell and touch began to return. Marcus felt how cold it was, the rain had picked up from a drizzle to a proper storm, the sun was setting and it was cold. The Drain hadn't helped either, the combination of the exhaustion and the manifestation of the effects of removing so much heat from his body, the cold was taking hold harder than it would have had he just forgotten a coat. He shivered and wrapped his arms around himself bracing against the cold. Marcus looked up and down the street for his next destination when a white utility van pulled up, brakes screeching as the rusted rear doors flew open.

A young, tall, well-built, brown haired man hopped out of the driver's seat and rushed around the van to him in jeans, flip flops, and a tight "Peace on Earth" t-shirt that showed off his muscles. One look at this guy and Marcus tried to make a run for it only to suddenly feel light headed, as if he were going to faint again.

"No no no no, none of that now," the man said as he

grabbed him from his stumbling fall and hoisted him into the back of the van. Marcus was too weak to fight back. "Don't worry, Marcus. You are going to be ok."

Marcus found he was also too weak to support himself as he was jostled around the back of the van turn after turn bouncing against walls and doors and dozens of potted plants in silent agony. The majority of his energy was spent on trying to see the man and where they were going but to little avail.

All he managed to creak out was, "Who are you?"

The van made a final turn and slammed to a stop, "I am Lance and I am here to help." the man said as he got out of his seat and climbed into the back.

Lance took a deep breath and started running his hands over Marcus' body. Marcus choked as a long stream of smoke was pulled out from his lungs by Lance's twirling fingers. He felt his nose clear out as well as more emissions continued to pour and ooze out of him. He was confused about what was happening and looked down at what Lance was doing. It looked like he was casting over Marcus, Lance's hands only a few inches from his tattered clothes, the air shimmered between them, light reflecting off the open spots on Marcus' shirt and onto Lance's pale arms.

"You don't have to..." Marcus started.

"Oh, don't worry, I do this all the time," Lance smiled, not looking away from what he was doing. His smile soothed Marcus, who was no longer feeling pain. In fact, it seemed as though he was no longer feeling any sort of effects of The

Drain. As his vision came together and the aches started to disappear, he looked around the van. It was nothing special, in fact it was dirty. The potted plants around him were all dead and leaves were scattered on the floor, five gallon buckets were tossed around and the floor was covered in dried paint.

"How are you doing this?" he asked, suddenly more comfortable.

"There will be plenty of time for that later," Lance said, removing his hands from Marcus and giving him a wink. "But I think you have a meeting to get to. I don't think anyone will be looking for you. Except... well don't worry about him just yet. I'm sure he won't come around."

"What? What meeting? Who is looking for me?" Marcus sputtered, pulling himself up to square off with Lance.

Lance used his considerable size and dominance in the van to herd Marcus out of the back doors, "See you around, bud!" he called as he tossed a zipped gym bag out the doors just before they closed and he sped off spewing dead leaves from the open windows.

Marcus unzipped the bag and looked inside. All that it contained was a set of clothes, which perfectly fit, and a pamphlet for Magic Anonymous, with a calendar of events. Marcus already had The Group calendar in his wallet but he didn't have that anymore.

Marcus stepped out onto the street to get his bearings. He immediately knew where he was. Lance had brought him to the parking structure of the Our Lady Eternal Community Center where Marcus had gone to his weekly Group meetings for the past three years. Marcus looked at his wrist for his watch. Instead of a watch, he found that he was covered in soot that was now streaking down his body in the rain. He ran across the street and into the wide stained glass double doors of the center and saw on the lobby clock that it would be another hour and a half until Group started. He had time to kill. Worse than that, he had time to think.

As he made his way through the center, he couldn't help but feel watched by the few people who were there, the memory of the day and the questions that he had turned to demons that gnashed their teeth into his consciousness and he could feel them following him into the building. Lance had somehow helped him with The Drain, but now his walk had turned into an emotional trudge as he made his way through the building and into the showers, hoping to clean off at least the visible evidence of his mistakes. The Center was mostly empty but the few staff there knew him by name and greeted him by name as he walked by. Fortunately, they knew him from Group and would respect his privacy, but if anyone from outside the Center had shared that this is where he went to Group, it was unlikely that he would find sanctuary in its walls. Again, his demons trilled their tongues in his ear, causing him to look back at the entry to see if anyone was there.

Marcus stripped down and got into the shower, doing his best to wipe off the now caked on smoke that insisted on lingering. The hot water only increased the smell that wafted in the steam with him. Surrounded by the very essence of his day, the particles burning as they ran into the, now likely infected, burn on his hand, Marcus finally broke down. Tears ran down his face, mixing in with the shower and taking more dirt with them. He was going to have to leave town, he had to find Wallace first and apologize. That would be what would fix everything, seeing her, he could explain. He had made some grievous errors in their relationship, he would get a better job like she had pushed him to, he would go back to school, maybe. There had to be something to fix it.

As the stranger's grin came back into his mind's eye, he had his first flicker of doubt followed by confusion. What had he called him? Why had he pulled him out of the apartment and saved him? Marcus lost track of his tears as the agony was replaced with a nauseating confusion. He ran naked from the showers to the closest bathroom stall and vomited into one of the toilets. A little red-haired head poked under the stall, laying on the disgusting floor. It was Mick.

"Ya' got the spins too, eh, Marcus?" He hiccuped in a drunken Irish slur, offering his flask up to Marcus, one eye barely open. Marcus could smell the booze on his breath. "Hair o' tha dag?"

"I'm good, Mick, thanks. You mind giving me a sec?" Marcus reached down and pushed Mick back to his stall by the top of his greasy knotted head of hair.

Mick was the kind of addict that most people wanted to try to avoid becoming. He had fallen into magic at a young age and fell down a spell hole pretty quickly. It had stunted his growth, leaving him at barely four and a half feet tall and, as he bounced between addictions, he had managed to pick up a bouquet of bad habits and a fractured reality, but everyone loved him. Despite the fact that his realities rarely aligned with everyone elses and that he couldn't be relied on to ever pay a debt, he had slept on every one of the regulars' couches when he needed a place and was clearly kind at heart, no matter how broken he was. He had become something of a mascot at Group.

"Suit yer'self, ya naked weirdo." He scoffed, glugging and gagging as he threw back whatever concoction was pushing the limits of his body's ability to keep him alive tonight.

Marcus pushed himself up through the fog of panic and back into the shower, now very conscious of his vulnerability, and his nudity, and spent the rest of his time before Group in the shower figuring out his next steps.

Chapter Three

By the time that six thirty rolled around, Marcus had a plan to leave town.

Step One: Find Wallace and apologize, show her that he could be good, show her the ring that was now stuck in his hand and tell her that he would make it all better and convince her to come with him.

Step Two: The normal routes to leave the city would be monitored. In the case of a violent casting, The Regulators would set up checkpoints to catch the caster in case they tried to flee. Marcus would have to rely on a little illusion work to make it out but he was sure that Wallace would be ok with it, it was their future after all. So in full disguise he would sneak as best he could past the magic detection and sneak his way on foot over the bridge.

Step Three: Once outside the city and off the island, Marcus and Wallace would get bus tickets, paid in cash, to the farthest farm town in the middle of nowhere and just go.

Marcus had visions of the future they had always talked about, living off the land with a fun escape montage running through his head. They would have chickens and fields of crops, maybe corn, maybe something a little more unique, a zucchini ranch or maybe a pumpkin patch that specialized in big Halloween events. Either way, they would escape together. Everything else would fall into place.

He made his way out of the bathroom, his loaner shirt, white with a big red heart "I Love New York", and jeans were dripping wet from not having a towel and each of his steps made a *SQUEECH!* sound as he walked down the hallway that yelled "Look at me! Something is off here!". As he made it to the auditorium doors, he peeked into the meeting area, people were just starting to trickle in. A golden retriever of a man with a bowl cut bounced around between greeting people and moving chairs into a circle. This was George Larratt, leader of Group and storyteller extraordinaire. Marcus made one last check for any strangers, hoping that none of The Regulators had made their way into information about which meetings he might be attending and, seeing none, slipped into the closest group that had circled around a coffee station. He poured himself a styrofoam cup of the sludge.

"No magic in this, eh?" A voice behind him made him jump and turn around. Looking behind him was a short brunette with a pixie cut. "You never said thank you, you know for saving your life?" It clicked, she was the woman who had grabbed him out of traffic earlier that day.

"I, um, thanks," he stammered. "Who..."

"I'm Diandra," she smiled, extending her hand for a very aggressively placed handshake. Marcus shook. "My friends call me Di."

"I haven't..." Marcus stammered, his hand still clenched in her surprisingly strong hands.

"Seen me here before? Yeah I hate these things, a whole bunch of self pity that really brings down my buzz." With an awkward pull Marcus was able to free himself from her.

"You know that's..."

"Yeah, offensive? Only for the soft folks. You soft, Marcus?" She poked him in the stomach, he was a little and it hurt, he hadn't realized how sore he was.

"Stop that!" he said flinching away.

The movement attracted George's attention who abandoned the last of the chairs that he was setting up and jogged over, "How's it going over here you two?" He said with his classic grin approaching with some sort of a dance shuffle that involved way too much hip but the right amount of finger pointing, "Marcus, I see you have met Di. She is, well she used to be a regular way back when."

"Until I found a different path," She smiled at George.

"I still think..." George started.

"That I should have kept coming? That I would have found a good influence? I think I have plenty of those now." She smiled and walked off, running her hand across Marcus' upper back and headed towards the few people who had sat down.

Marcus watched her walk away and when she was as a safe distance leaned into George, "Is she always like that?"

George hadn't recovered entirely and was still staring at her. "Quick to interrupt and rude? Seems like forever since she was anything else. You know I knew her when she was easier to be around." His face had grown serious, a look that Marcus had rarely seen on his 'beacon of support' as he called it, just for a second though and then he snapped back to his smile, "But have no fear, she grows on you." and he walked away.

"Not that I'll have to worry about that," Marcus muttered almost disappointed that he would never see George again.

"What was that?" George said over his shoulder, pausing for a moment to look back.

"Nothing," Marcus called back and headed over to the circle.

George called out for the meeting to start and the rest of the lingering crowd found their seats. The majority of the regular drawn faces were there. Most people at Group were not as lucky as Marcus had been, they had never been caught and forced to any sort of rehabilitation program, most of them were regular users and the effects of the Drain had left them looking more like corpses than humans, unresponsive to more than basic requests. All of them except for Di. In the circle of cadaver toned skin, she glowed and smiled with perfectly white teeth, not a patch of dry skin or a bag under her eye. She had to be a tourist. There was no way that she was really a magic user.

Mick hopped up into the folding chair next to Marcus and fell asleep against his arm as George started off with the M.A. opening, a few voices, including Marcus followed along out loud in a broken, but rehearsed, unison, "We are here to be better, we are Magic addicts, brothers and sisters in a craft that creates shortcuts to pain, not to happiness. We do not stop being addicts because we stop using magic. We are always healing, always better, always willing to work to find the right path to happiness."

As George continued with reading a passage from the Magicians Anonymous Codex, their book to a spell free life, Marcus watched Di from across the circle. She pulled out a Codex from her bag, it was filled with post-its and tags, from where he sat, he could see highlighting and notes scribbled throughout the well worn book and there was tape holding the spine together. She pulled a long feather quill from her bag and started scribbling notes as Geoge went on. Marcus was transfixed by her and this bizzare display.

Di looked up at him and smirked, winked, and then went back to whatever she was doing. There was something about that smirk that Marcus found familiar, something that irked him beyond his regular distaste for tourists. So many non-casting people loved coming to Group to see the people who were casters. Most of them would either pretend to be addicts themselves or have a loved one who they wanted to understand better. Once in, a good number of them would go as far as to try to goad some of them into performing a spell for them, either for gain or for the mere entertainment of it. Most non-addicts didn't care about the Drain once they had a taste of the power that magic held.

"Turning tricks", as it was called by the community, was the way most of them ended up where they were. In most cases, casters started because they were interested in magic, whether for fun or for profit, people would take advantage of them. Magician Bum Fights had hundreds of millions of online views and most addicts couldn't get jobs once they were on the registry so they would risk their lives on spells for some cash. This is where tourists came in. They would attend meetings, pretending to be an addict and then indoctrinate a weak minded addict into whatever job they were trying to pull. But George saw her, he wouldn't allow a non-user to sit in and risk dragging one of his flock back in or deeper into addiction. Who was she? If not a wolf in sheep's clothing, she had to be an addict, but she was too clean. She was...

"... Marcus?" George's voice finally made it through the fog of Marcus' focus. Marcus shook his head, clearing his mind, and pivoted to George, "I believe today is a special day for you?"

Marcus had been pulled back to a harsh reality, he tried to think of what to say but only got out a stammer. He thumbed the ring in his palm, hoping that it would give him some sort of strength and clarity to come up with how to explain that on the day celebrating his third year of sobriety he had relapsed, nearly killing dozens of people in his apartment. He managed a shrug as his eyes fell to the ground.

Di chimed in, "If Golden Boy isn't ready to speak, I am ready to share." Marcus' stomach churned and he winced, it was painful to even hear her happy voice from his place of agony.

"I don't think that now is appropriate, Di" George said, perhaps a little more forcefully than he probably intended. But the intensity of his response lifted a few of the others out of whatever daydreams they had slipped into and placed their interest on the edge of their seats.

"I think now is a perfect time, George." She smiled back, leaning forward and looking up out of the top of her eyes, and stood up. "My name is Di, and I am an *addict*." the word addict hit her lips with a disdain that felt like another stab at Marcus.

"Hello, Di," the circle echoed. Marcus noticed that George didn't join in.

"Gosh, it has been so long since I have seen some of you." her eyes rested on George, "For the most part, I don't expect you to remember me, so I'll start at the beginning. I have been an addict for twenty years, and today, like yesterday, and the day before, I relapsed."

"That's a... that's the spu'rit," Mick slurred, resting his head on Marcus' lap as he slipped back into unconsciousness.

"Thanks," she chuckled, rolling her eyes. "Anyway, I have been an addict since I was a little kid. My bio dad went off to fight someone else's war and after he found death on the end of a stick, my mother found herself Hank. He was, well, most of us would call him a bad dude. He was a pretty big fan of slapping ol' Mom around and then coming after me. Mom was sure it was because we had done something wrong so we lived by the Law of Hank." With that last bit she rolled her wrist in the air and struck a very proper pose, holding her hand up like she was serving her words on a platter. "It didn't take too long for Hank to have a brilliant thought, why not make a little extra dough by getting his new step-daughter into the wonderful world of magic. It started slow, introducing me to some hedge witches, then going to temples here and there, sharing stories of great magicians throughout the ages. Making them out to be heroes. I was groomed to become his little bank of magic favors. As the beatings continued and the magic got stronger, in a spell gone terribly right, Hank died and Mom and I were free. Or at least we would have been if Mom hadn't decided that that was the biggest crime since Prometheus stole fire, she ran out and ratted me out. I almost got caught too, but I ran, and in getting by with a little help from my friends, here I am."

George spoke through clenched teeth, "Thank you, Di. As per the usual, it would be greatly appreciated if we could work towards remorse and repentance for our past sins. *Murder* included."

"Of course, George, I will work on that." Di gave a little bow and sat back down in her chair. Marcus stared, she had just admitted to murder, she had to know that that would be reported by someone in Group, George had a legal obligation, even in cases of self defense. Group was anonymous and was a safe place from all things except intent to cause damage to yourself or others, or previous crimes in which someone had been injured. She had to know that.

"How about you, Marcus?" George was back to beaming in a way that pleaded for any sort of salvation, "How are you today?"

Marcus forced himself up to his feet, this would be difficult, "Hi, I'm Marcus and I'm an addict."

"Hi, Marcus." Everyone echoed back, but he heard Di's voice over the others, she had locked eyes with him and stared, unblinking at him, and he couldn't help but maintain that same locked gaze. The world melted around them as he spoke, as if he were only speaking to her.

"Today was supposed to be the best day of my life so far. I was supposed to get engaged today," he choked on the words, "but Wallace, most of you know Wallace, she had someone else." he did his best to shake back the tears but they were inevitable. "Today was also supposed to be my third year of sobriety, three years clean since I met her, three years since I had any trouble with the Regulators," someone in the circle spat on the ground at their name, but Marcus wasn't breaking eye contact with Di, "and then today, *for the first time in three years,* I relapsed."

He started to sit down, but Di interrupted even that, "What happened, that's not a story, we're here to heal, right? Come on, full story, man!"

"That's enough, Di," George snapped, "The man is

hurting, we take things at our own pace here. Thank you, Marcus, for..."

"There will be a lot more hurting for him in the future if he doesn't learn to get over the crap he gets himself into. Let's hear it, Marcus!"

"Di!"

Marcus straightened up, "It's fine, George." He had no idea where this strength was coming from, but he wasn't going to let this stranger take him down. "I've got this. You want to know who I am, fine. You weren't the only one with a sad story," He gestured to the burn on his ear, "some of us didn't even have the pleasure of being able to blame a stepdad. My real dad liked to drink, drank my mom into an early grave. Then again, it could have been that fall down the stairs, probably was actually an accident too, right? Just like I was. My dad never let me forget that that was who I was to him, an accident. He said that I was the reason she died. I was the albatross around his neck."

He paused, trying to find reason in rage and found himself back in his story. "I started using magic when I fell in with a group of kids who just wanted to try something dangerous, just for a break from normal life. We were all friends, it started with a few tricks to have better lives, but nothing ever made my life better, I always went home to him. When I turned 15 I left home, turning tricks on the street to survive. I had a small apartment with a few of my friends, we all bounced around and from job to job until we got caught or ended up in jail. Some of us made it out, I thought I did when I got caught on my 25th birthday stealing a cake and liquor, a damn vanishing spell that failed, chased into a cook house that ended in three blocks burning down. I got sent to the rehab where I met Wallace. But then today happened. I guess I'm an addict for life. I should know that by now. We all are. " Marcus shrugged, and sat down, still glaring at Di.

Before he could get into his seat though, he landed on something soft that screamed, "Ger'rof me, you spoon!" It was Mick who had apparently laid down into Marcus' chair as he was speaking. Marcus pushed him up, accidentally squeezing a plume of gas out of him, and back into his own seat before sitting down.

"Thank you, Marcus." George said, "I am so sorry that you are going through this." his gaze set on Di. "Wallace seemed so nice, we need to realize that our strength and reason for quitting needs to come from within, because any of the pain or strength from the world around us is only temporary. Support is important, but can be fickle. We need to build our strength one day at a time." He smiled supportively.

Di took a deep breath and placed her hands together over her mouth, sighing a dramatic yawn. "Do you think maybe you aren't taking enough of the blame though?"

Marcus felt ill trying to keep his rage down, "Excuse me?"

"Di, don't do this," George started.

"No no no, not a big thing, just trying to heal here," Di continued, waving George off, "Really, think about it. Your dad was a jerk, your mom was dead, your friends were bad influences, your girlfriend cheated, did you ever think that it might just be that you aren't good enough? All of your story happened to you, you didn't take a stand in any of that. Not for a moment of your life did you sound like you took control. Could that be because you are too weak to take what is yours?" She leaned in as if she was expecting a revelation to be cast forward into Marcus.

"I..." Marcus stammered "Who do you think you are?" He felt himself starting to get hot, like he was going to burst into flames hot. Di must have noticed, her eyes grew wide for a second in surprise.

"Whoa, there Golden Boy, just asking a question!" She chuckled, throwing up two hands in surrender. "I didn't mean to offend. I just wanted to dig deeper. You know? Help the healing"

George got up to his feet and stepped into the middle of the circle, "Maybe it is time that we move onto anyone else. Would ANYONE else like to speak or have a story to share?" he pleaded but nobody moved, this was the most interesting a meeting had been and for once, all eyes were on what was going on. George gave up on trying to get someone else to speak but did not leave the middle of the circle, physically blocking Marcus from seeing Di.

"Ok well if we don't have any more testimony to give, I'll wrap this meeting up a little early. Di, I will need to speak with you before you go, Marcus, you too. Tomorrow night, for those of you who would like to join us, I will be discussing chapter seven in the Codex on spirituality and strength. We will end tonight with our hearts open to healing and our hopes open for Marcus and Di, who have found hard times on the road to recovery, may you two find your way back to the safe path of healing." He looked Marcus in the eyes, "We are all here for you." and gave him a nod. "Now if any of you would be so interested, my wife made us brownies tonight, they are truly magical." He laughed, "but seriously, they are delicious and there is no magic in them."

With a clap of his hands, he released everyone to their evenings and, as everyone stood up, Marcus scanned the group for Di ready to give her a piece of his mind. He spotted her making her way towards the coffee and brownies but as he started towards her. A hand grabbed his shoulder, it was George.

"Listen, Marcus, how are you doing, bud?" He was tall and bowed his head a little to get at eye level with Marcus, as if he were a parent speaking with a hurt child. "Do you need anything?"

"I'm fine, George, thank you." Marcus forced a smile and tried to shrug it off, he didn't want to lose the emotional intensity he had ready for Di. "I think I just need to spend some time thinking about who I am and why I am healing." He checked again, Di was stacking brownies on a plate. He tried to step around George and the conversation that was starting, but George got in his way putting another supporting and firm hand on Marcus' shoulder.

"Di can be a real pain, before you started coming, she was a regular, but give her time. She takes a lot of her own pain and puts it on others, it is her way of coping. She calls it 'passing the ball'. We are working on her not using the ball as a bludgeon to hurt others. She is just a little slow on the uptake. I really shouldn't admit it but you two are two of my favorites, take some time to get to know her. You two would be great resources for each other. Don't let hate win, Marcus. Try peace with others and you might find it for yourself."

"Sure thing, George. Thanks." Marcus was ready for a fight if only he could get around him and, sure enough, George let go and Marcus made a bee line over to Di.

Before he could get there, Di turned and faced him, "You know his wife doesn't make these?" She said, frowning at the plate in her hands, brownies stacked three tall covering the styrofoam, the plate bowing under the weight of the stolen desserts.

Marcus stopped in his tracks at a complete loss, "What?" was all that fell out of his mouth.

"George used to make these every meeting, he took a ton of pride in them until one of the attendees made fun of him for enjoying baking. He didn't stop making them, but then would just say that his wife made them. They are some of the best brownies you will ever have, here!" she stretched out her arms, offering her plate which now had nearly two-thirds of all of the brownies from the original tray.

Marcus took one as he was trying to gather his thoughts. He was expecting her to lead in with another attack and now his planned and rehearsed opening line wouldn't make any sense.

She continued, "Sorry about that before, George has let me know that I can come off as a little abrasive. That I alienate myself from others by forcing my own insecurities on them or some crap like that. What do you say I grab you a coffee and you walk me home? My place is just on the other side of the park. I hate walking in the park alone at night." she smiled a chocolatey smile that made Marcus think of a small child asking for a toy.

Marcus was completely floored, he didn't have the cruelty in him to fight her after an apology, she even seemed to mean it. George vouched for her and Marcus trusted him. "Sure, I don't have anywhere else to be anyway." he said, trying to sound as cool as possible, "It's a nice night for a walk anyway."

Di poured two cups of coffee, handing Marcus one, and, with a few goodbyes to other attendees, they headed out the door into the cold dark drizzle, Marcus more confused now than when he had gotten there. His plans for what to do next swirled around him and were lost again in the rain as the two of them started towards Central Park.

Chapter Four

Di was ahead of Marcus by a few steps so he jogged up to keep pace. For someone so short she kept a quick pace as she balanced the plate of brownies on top of her cup of coffee, "Gods, these are good!" she said, grabbing her third brownie and putting it in her mouth whole, never missing a step.

"I think George meant for those to be shared," Marcus said, embarrassed by how quickly he had managed to lose his breath.

"I left some!" she laughed defensively, her mouth full of brownie. She paused and took a sip of the coffee, "Ugh! They are almost enough to make up for this swill." and spat it back into the cup, then proceeded to pour it out onto the sidewalk and threw the cup into a bin as they walked past. "No magic in that, for sure!" she laughed again.

Marcus stepped around the new brown cloud of a puddle on the ground and continued their pace. She was a difficult personality, he was already starting to realize how long this walk was going to be.

"So how long have you been going to group?" She asked, picking her way into another chocolate lump, the rain starting to get to them.

"Three years this time around," Marcus said, a little put off by the fact that she didn't seem to remember that from his story no more than fifteen minutes earlier, "I have had problems with self control leading to the abuse of destructive magic!"

"That suuuucks!" she craned her head back as she said it, "I couldn't imagine being an addict for that long!"

Marcus let it roll off, "How about you? How long have you..."

"Been casting? It feels like forever," she interrupted, it seemed to be her default conversation style. "Sorry about your dog. How long did you have it?"

"My dog?" he said, totally lost.

"Isn't that why you relapsed? I think I blanked out during your story."

"You mean my girlfriend?"

"Eh, a bitch is a bitch am I right?" she looked back over her shoulder at him and shrugged innocently. Marcus really felt like agreeing but held off at the risk of pointing out any irony. Di smacked her mouth, as she eyed the brownies again and opened her mouth up towards the sky trying to catch some rain. It was more than a little disgusting.

"You know, I know a good place to get coffee just around the corner, we could stop in there if you want something to drink." Marcus offered, "A few of us go there after meetings usually and grab a cup, if you are thinking about rejoining Group, building a support base really has helped me with my recovery."

"Clearly," Di responded, her tone once again irking Marcus. "But I'm not here to make friends, the pickings are slim and the whole victim complex of addiction is a real turn off." Her words were cold and judgey for someone who had met her present company at an addiction meeting that she had chosen to attend because of admitted abuse.

They made it the rest of the way to Central Park in silence, her upbeat steps were barely tolerable. Marcus couldn't imagine how so many years of The Drain had left her upright. That is assuming she wasn't just lying through her perfectly white teeth, which Marcus was starting to suspect had to be fake. She should be way more like Mick and be a husk of the person she was if she had been as heavy a caster as she had claimed to be, not hopping through the faded chalk of that day's hopscotch games on the sidewalk.

He had been so focused on Di that he had nearly forgotten that he had burnt down the life that he had built for himself that afternoon, but as he rolled his ankle on a crack it all came rushing back. The cold wind blew and he realized that not only was he wearing a borrowed shirt from a stranger that had rescued him from the Regulators, but that he was also on borrowed time. He had to get to Wallace and start the process of escaping the city. At this point the Regulators had to be closing in and it was unlikely that he would have more than another 24 hours before any of their tracking spells were able to catch up with him.

"Are we almost there?" The question was instinctual and unnecessary, Marcus had been blindly following Di, at night, in an empty park, he had no idea where he was. Looking up, he could just make out the Met and realized that he was on East Drive.

"Just about," her answer sounded deliberately short. Di looked back at Marcus and smiled, "It's just up here."

They cut across a path in front of the Met towards the Obelisk and that is when Marcus felt an uneasy sensation run down his back. He heard a shuffle behind him and looked over his shoulder instinctually and saw as a man stood up from behind some bushes and started towards them.

Probably a homeless man, "Sorry, man. We don't have anything!" Marcus yelled back. He felt for the homeless, he had been there a few times throughout his addiction when his friends would kick him out over not sharing a spell he had figured out.

"Now why'd you have to do that?" Di hissed, grabbing his hand in hers and dropping the plate, "We have to go!"

She pulled on him hard as she coaxed him into a run.

"What are you talking about? The guy is probably looking for some change." Marcus resisted but Di had a pretty strong grip and was pulling hard. Then a whistle broke the silence of the park, it was a single low tone coming from the man behind them. After a few moments, it should have stopped, but without taking a breath, the tone continued. That's when a chill ran down Marcus' spine and he gave into the run.

The low tone was joined by another, and then another, the whistles surrounding them. Di pulled Marcus down next to a bench into a clump of bushes.

"What are we doing? What the hell is..." Marcus said.

"Shh!" Di hissed, half covering his mouth with her hand and half slapping him.

"We should keep going! Who are they?"

"For the love of the Gods, be quiet!" Di snapped, poking her head up to look around. "There isn't anywhere to run, they knew we would be here."

"Who knew..."

"Does quiet mean nothing to you! You are going to get yourself killed all over again!" She squatted back down and grabbed him by the shoulders, "Be ready to fight."

"What do you mean fight?" Marcus asked.

Di started muttering rhythmically, wringing her hands

together.

"What are you doing?"

"What part of shut up don't you understand?" She snapped back, her hands started to glow blue.

"Seriously! What the hell is going on! Do you have any idea..."

"I'm seriously sick of your questions, sweetie!" Her voice changed to calm, "Poke your head out there and see if they are still following us."

Marcus poked his head out and was able to make out five silhouettes, no more than twenty yards away, running towards them.

"They're still there." he whispered, crouching back down with her.

"Good," she smiled and pushed him full force into the sidewalk causing him to tumble to the ground.

As he stood up he was face to face with one of the men, if you could even call it that. The creature that he was looking at was a human, except a few very disturbing features. It had no eyes, just open sockets, its mouth was sewn shut, and its skin was just barely hanging onto his face. Next to it on either side stood another four of the same almost identical things, effectively blocking any sort of escape that he had. Even without eyes, Marcus felt their gaze on him. He cautiously pushed himself to his feet, his hands up in trying to be as visibly non-threatening as possible.

They all stood there for a moment, as much as they could staring at each other. Marcus felt like nothing was going to happen when a voice started from all five of them simultaneously. Emitting from their closed mouths which only added to the terror of the situation.

"We have been looking for you for a long time, Ra'Saram," the voice said, creating a harmony with itself, "I am sorry that I could not be here to greet you in person and instead had to send my golems, but as I am sure you could imagine, I wanted to take the time to do this one last time. To really make it special."

Di stepped out from behind the bench, her arms outstretched in an exaggerated shrug, a bright blue light illuminating the park around them, "Sorry Kallis, no Ra'Saram here, looks like your golems were mistaken. No biggie!"

"Ahh, Di. I should have known you would be here," the voice started to sound familiar to Marcus. As it continued to speak a long, wafting, cloud of black smoke seeped out from between the stitches in the golems' mouths, little seams of lightning crackling inside of it, forming into a big head that floated in the middle of them. In the blue light the features weren't perfectly defined but the face was unmistakable, it was the man that had been with Wallace that afternoon. "Hello again, Marcus. It is nice to see you again."

Marcus felt the fire burning inside of him again and his hands began glowing. He took a swing at the head and his hands passed straight through. "Whoa there, buddy! Nice try but I'm a floating head made of smoke, what made you think that would work? No wonder Wallace lost interest in you! Quite the brain trust."

"Don't you dare say her name!" Marcus yelled, his arms pulsing.

"It would probably be nice to see her again wouldn't it? How about we make a deal. My golems kill you, she watches, and then she gets to walk out of here. Wallace, honey, there's a call for you." As the head spoke it started to morph into another figure, before it had solidified, Marcus already knew who it was going to be, Wallace appeared, clearly tied to a chair.

Small smoke tears ran down her face, dropping to the ground and rippling out towards his feet, "Marcus, I'm so..." her eyes opened wide and a choking croak came out of her mouth. With each gasp she spat out a bit more smoke, but she could not seem to form any words.

"Running out of time, buddy!" The man's voice joined back in. Marcus stared in horror as he watched the smoke figure of Wallace choke, "Your call, her or you."

"Help... me..." Wallace choked, the lightning in her neck becoming red and angry as it crackled with her voice.

"Fine! Kill me, just let her go!" Marcus' voice cracked as he stared into Wallace's frantic eyes.

The man laughed as Marcus watched Wallace kick and struggle trying to gasp for breath, after a few moments, her head spun with a sickening snap and she went limp.

"That gets me every time, Marcus!" The man laughed, "That was too much fun! It really is too bad we don't get to do this more often." the smoke shifted back into the head and winked. "I guess you're up!"

The smoke flew back into the golems and they leapt back to life, their eye sockets erupting into a purple light, "For the last time, Ra'Saram, goodbye!" they said.

The middle golem lunged towards Marcus arms outstretched, into sharpened nails that aimed at his chest but Di dove into its side, pushing her entire weight against it like a 5'4" linebacker. She climbed up its body, gripping to its head as she screamed. Blue light flowed down her arms into its head. Its sockets burst wide with blue light and its lips split open into a silent scream, the stitches in its mouth splitting its lips to ribbons as it then crumpled to the ground with Di landing in a crouch over it.

The two to the right stepped back and bent sideways towards each other, arms outstretched, making a circle between them, and a ball of red energy crackled between their arms and between their almost touching fingertips, a gale force wind building from behind them kicking up leaves and debris towards Marcus.

Marcus planted his feet and focused all of his energy into his hands, summoning flames that engulfed his fists. He launched himself forward and started swinging, one hand landing square on the jaw of the first golem launching it across the walkway and into a tree where it hit with a crunching thud, its body limp and lifeless.

The second one was already fighting Di, the two of

them were diving from cover to cover shooting bolts of crackling magic at each other. Di managed to land a bolt on the leg of the golem and immediately charged in leaping forward landing a glowing blue punch in its gut and as it crumpled she launched herself over its head grabbing it by the eye sockets and with one fluid motion bringing her knee to the back of its head and with a sickening crunch, snapped its neck.

As Marcus turned to find the other two he saw that they had also started making their own ball of red light. They shifted their feet and swung their arms around to point at Marcus, the orb following the path that their arms guided. He braced himself, he had never fought using magic and had only seen a few underground magic fights, but knew that they almost always ended in someone dying, with the day he was having, he more than welcomed it. He started to lift his arms to cover his face when he was thrown through the air by an invisible force, landing on the grass ten feet away.

He rolled and looked to see as George stepped in front of the ball his hands held together like he was in prayer, but with his fingers pointing forwards towards the ball, taking the full force of the energy, it pushed him back, sliding his feet along the ground, and wisps of red electricity crackled throughout his body, "Not this time, Kallis!" He yelled and the yell grew to a roar as the energy crackled down into his fingertips and he sent it back at the two golems, a beam tearing holes through both of their chests and they collapsed.

Marcus was dazed, he had never used magic in such a short period before and on top of the effects of The Drain he was completely spent, "What... was... that..." he panted as he struggled to push himself up to his feet.

Di looked around quickly and she reached out, her hand glowing with a white light and touched the forehead of the golem, "He's gone, you're safe for now." She looked at George, "We've got to go."

Marcus took a step and crumpled to the sidewalk and darkness started to overtake him. He could just make out Di running towards him and he felt her hands running over his body.

"It doesn't seem like he has any injuries. Every freaking time... he always pulls from his own energy. Don't tell me you're going to make me carry him myself! I swear I'll use him if you do."

George stood over him, and started lifting him up. "We need to get him out of here, there will be more on their way."

"I told you he was ready," Di said, standing over him smiling and Marcus lost consciousness to The Drain.

Chapter Five

When Marcus came to, he was floating in a vast blue expanse, a clear light blue wrapping around him and a soft breeze pushing him. He felt light and the warmth of the sunless sky bathed his skin in a protective calm. As he stretched he realized that the blue was not the sky, but rather some sort of cloth. From outside this cocoon he heard voices and laughter. Suddenly he was overcome with panic, the realization that he was alive and that he was wrapped in some kind of shroud.

"I'm alive! Wait!" he screamed, pushing his arms up to try and break through whatever tarp he was wrapped in and he kicked his legs throwing himself up and out as he tumbled out of a parachute hammock as he hit the ground, the blue cloth happy to be rid of his weight as it blew away revealing his surroundings.

Looking around, he was sitting on a hill, overlooking what appeared to be some kind of ranch, a few dozen people walking around down below. A few feet away, a group of three children jumped back as he fell and they laughed at him as he tried to regain the breath that had been knocked out of him in the fall.

"You sure are, Mr. Marcus. Alive and well." One of the children, a young boy of maybe eight or nine, said. "My name is Liam. I am supposed to watch you until you wake up." He put his hands on his hips proud of having a job.

"Then what?" asked Marcus.

"I dunno, nobody told me anything." Liam said.

"Where am I?" Marcus asked, trying to get his bearings. From the hilltop, he couldn't see any part of the city, just forest for miles around this large clearing. He pushed himself up and the children scattered, running down the hill to the others. "Where are you go..." he started, then shouting after them yelled "Where am I?"

From behind him he heard a voice, "You are safe, Marcus. We call this place The Ranch. It's simple, I know, it is a place of protection and learning." The voice belonged to George, who walked up next to him and gestured out to a farmhouse and barn sitting just inside the valley below. "We bring promising magic users here to help them hone their craft."

"Like a school for magic?" Marcus scoffed, still trying to take in where he was.

"I would love to say that this is a school, but that might be a bit reductive. I would say it is more of a guerrilla training camp for magic. But not in the dictator overthrowing things kind of way, this is a nicer place. So more like... I can't believe I didn't have a better introduction for this place, just so much going on. This is a training ranch for magic. There we go! A secret magic bed and breakfast in which people learn to use and fight using magic."

"Ok," Marcus wasn't any less confused, "Where are we? Do you steal the children?" he was getting a bit more brazen, a bit more accusational with his questions. George's kindness suddenly seemed sinister.

"Oh Gods no!" George laughed appalled, "The children came with their families voluntarily, some were adopted from foster care before coming here. We have plenty of adults here as well! Nothing evil, man. We are the good guys!" George was clearly offended but had to scramble for a response. He took a second and recomposed himself. "We are in upstate New York, this place belongs to Mick and his family, passed down generation to generation since before the conquistadores even learned to sail."

Marcus was out of things to say, he was more than dumbstruck by this whole new world around him. As Marcus looked beyond the immediate group around him he noticed that there appeared to be even more people who were throwing beach ball-sized air pockets back and forth. They ran and laughed as little disruptions of air flew around them at alarming speeds. Occasionally one person would miss the catch and be thrown off their feet by a great amount of force a few dozen feet through the air, tumbling and landing safely on the ground. To another side of them there was a basketball court where a group of teens were shooting hoops. It was a variation of the game horse but instead of all the teens being gathered around the basket that they were targeting they all were on the other half of the court. One of the girls in the group grabbed the ball from a taller boy, took three running steps and launched herself from half-court to dunk the ball. The taller boy that she had grabbed the ball from stood his mouth agape as the others cheered. A few followed in suit but only a few of them were able to make the jump.

George broke the silence already knowing what was going through Marcus' head, "We figured out how to safely cast with minimal effects of the Drain. It's one of the reasons that we chose this place. It's so full of life that we always have the source to feed off," he laughed as his explanation clearly didn't clear any shock from Marcus's face. "The entire concept is called Channeling. Here watch."

He picked up a stick that had fallen from the tree above, it was nothing more than a twig with a couple of leaves still attached and a few small seed pods. He took the seed pods, pushed them into the ground, and hovered his hand a few inches off the ground and the ground started to rumble as the dirt split as a flurry of leaves fell from the trees above and within the matter of seconds a full tree stood between them. Marcus looked around expecting a group gathered at such a sight but at this point even the group that had been watching him had dispersed. George took his hands and wiped them off on his pants and placed them on Marcus's shoulders, "I had enough power to do that because

I pulled the power from somewhere else, look at the other trees."

Marcus looked up around him. The trees that held the hammock had lost nearly half of their leaves but, despite that, didn't seem any worse for the wear. "All power comes from somewhere, Marcus. Part of what we teach here is learning how to borrow that power from the things around us in a safe way so that we can make the world a better place. I would like to teach you that power so that the next time that you come up against Kallis you will be better prepared for the fight." His eyes got dark and he maintained eye contact with Marcus and his hands tightened on his shoulders. "We need you for this. We need all of you for this. Without you we will all die and if you aren't ready to commit we might as well give up now."

This was the most serious that Marcus had ever seen George. He had listened to stories, while in Group, about the years of abuse and how he had seen people die in the streets from the Drain, he had traveled the world and seen some of the greatest suffering but even when he told those stories George was never one to break from a smile of encouragement and yet there he stood lips pursed, brow furrowed and not an ounce of comfort to give. Then, like the sun breaking through a storm, a smile emerged, "So if this is the path that you would like to be on, I figure we should start by *growing* your abilities."

Di poked her head out from behind the tree behind George, "BOOOOO!" she echoed through cupped hands only stopping once her hands were right next to George's ear. George's smile broadened, his signature dimples creasing as he grabbed Di and bent her backwards for a big kiss. Marcus stood there, just getting more confused.

"So," George said, straightening back up, "welcome to our home!"

Marcus looked at them,completely lost by the kiss, looking beyond them for answers and he found nothing.

George continued."I hate to put too much of a rush on this, but it is a little important that we do push forward, we have a bit of a schedule to keep."

Marcus searched for words, "This is a bit... much..." They weren't the words he was looking for, but summed up his position well enough.

"Oh you think this is a bit much," Di laughed, "Just wait until you actually find..."

"Di!" George interrupted, "give the man some room to build up an understanding. Yes, Marcus, this is a lot. Essentially, the magic that you know is a lie. It is a lie that has been perpetrated by the Gods for a long time to keep magic as a more... let's say 'divine' pursuit." He said the last part with air quotes and everything, rolling his eyes up at the sky as if he were speaking directly with the Gods themselves. "It is something that we learned only in the last millennia and have been working to perfect. I wouldn't say that we are there yet, but at least we have gotten channeling down well enough to try and teach it to a few promising casters."

Marcus wasn't broken from his stupor by George's words, he was still trying to figure out how he had even gotten to the hill that he was standing on when, for the first time in nearly a day, Wallace came to mind, "Can we save Wallace?" he said the words and knew the answer by Di and George's fallen faces.

"Marcus," Di walked up and put her hand on his shoulder, providing a comfort that he didn't think she was capable of, "she was dead long before that fight in the street and good riddance am I right? Talk about a distraction." Just like that the comfort was gone.

"For the love of..." George said, "Marcus, Kallis is the champion of evil, hand selected by the Gods to prove that the human experiment and the idea that we could handle magic would result in nothing but hate and destruction, he is the embodiment of all of the worst things that have ever happened in human history. One death, no matter how close to you it might be, can't matter. Moving on will be the only way to get to where we need to be."

Marcus felt the heat rising in him as George spoke, the flames building up and begging to be unleashed, "Don't talk about her like that." He growled, unsure of what he would do if it came to blows with these two, but he was ready to go, regardless.

"That will be one of the first things that we need to address," Di said, "your rage will be the biggest hurdle in victory, you were never like this before." she shook her head disapprovingly.

"Before?"

George stepped in again, Marcus was starting to

realize that George was acting as a physical censor to Di and that if he wanted to get more answers, he would need to get them more directly, but before he could demand them George continued.

"We have a lot to discuss, this is not going to be easy, but I need you to know, we are your biggest advocates, we always have been. You are destined to be great, just hang tight, come with us for a little tour and see what we are talking about."

Marcus had enough of a foothold in his new reality that walking behind the two as they led him down the hill was not overly difficult, but getting a feel for his surroundings was far from simple. Beyond the kids playing basketball, there was a group of adults, lined up in a formation like tai chi in the park, their arms flowing back and forth guiding a series of kites through the air, diving and spinning around like a flurry of large leaves, diving at unnatural angles and then soaring back up into the sky, unhindered by string. Alongside them, a smaller group of adults faded from invisible to opaque and back again, giving each other high fives and trying again.

To the other side of the court, Marcus could see a group that had circled up, they were cheering and a man and a child stood in the middle.

Marcus gestured over to them, "What's going on there."

Di stopped their silent march and let out a deep belly laugh, "Oh you'll love this! That's sparring. Most combat magic is very controlled here, restricted to only a few users

71

who are the most adept casters, who get to put on demonstrations.. It is quite the event to see. Come on!"

She grabbed his hand and pulled him quickly to the circle, pushing up towards the front. On his way past the few dozen people, he realized that they were all smiling and healthy, hardly the faces he had come to know to be associated with magic. It was uncomfortable for Marcus, being in a crowd of people doing magic, an act that he had considered to be a crime, out in the open. Not a single one showed any negative side effects. That blew his mind, but what was at the center of the circle, when he got to the inner ring, was what really put him over the top.

Standing in the center was an old man, probably in his late seventies, with long gray mutton chops, a floppy plaid buret, a kilt and a loose white shirt, holding a walking stick and wearing wooden clogs, squaring off against another man who Marcus had mistaken as a child. It was Mick.

Mick was, true to fashion, in an apparent stupor, but there was something controlled about his stumbling. He swayed back and forth in exaggerated motions as the crowd cheered. His arms waved back and forth, keeping balance as his feet touched the ground only long enough to start movement in the next one.

Di stepped out into the ring, her voice suddenly booming, "Alright everyone, we know the rules! No permanent disfigurement, no death, and no outside interference! Both fighters need to stay inside the circle at all times and must have enough control to not hit anyone standing outside the ring! First combatant to get knocked out of the ring or just knocked out loses. Mick, Charles, are you ready?" Both of the men nodded. "Awesome! Then let's get this started!" She threw her hands up towards the sky, a series of sparks and loud bangs erupting from her fingertips, and she dove for the side of the circle as Mick and Charles started circling each other.

Charles, who had seemed to rely heavily on the stick to keep his rotund form upright, straightened up, his rosy face getting rosier as he banged the stick on the ground once, twice, three times and an orb or purple energy crackled at the top. With a swift swing he hurled the ball at Mick who swung himself around it and pointed two fingers at Charles shooting a white crackling lightning at him. The old man spun his stick in front of him, shooting the electricity into the air around him, creating an orb that circled above him and hovered in the air, not dissipating.

Mick chuckled, "Interesting, old man, but that won't be enough."

Mick rolled his body around in an arc that made Marcus uneasy with how flexible the little drunk was as he brought both of his hands out in front of him, meeting them at the wrists and flaring his fingers outwards. With a pulling motion, each hand gliding down from wrist to elbow of the opposite hand then repeating again, he started pulling the orb into himself, spindles of power jumping from Charles and into Mick. Mick was pushed backwards as the electricity hit him, but he kept his footing and he stood, panting. His clothes were smoking with little holes from where the spindles hit him.

Charles threw three missiles of white light at him. Mick

quickly deflected those into the sky, creating a loud eruption overhead and an even louder eruption from the crowd. Applause and yells filled the air and Mick rallied, he leapt forward, dodging back and forth as Charles threw more smaller balls of red and yellow and blue at him. Mick launched himself over the last attack and grabbed onto Charles' staff. The crowd gasped.

Di leaned over to Marcus and whispered, "It is a combat faux-pa to grab another casters staff." She chuckled, "But all is fair in combat, a little pocket sand has been known to make an entrance in these games."

Marcus hadn't blinked for the entire fight, watching these two old men casting was like a miracle to him, a ballet with explosions. Mick started a low growl that grew to a yell as, like with the electricity before, a rainbow of color started erupting from the staff and pouring over him. When the source of the light changed to Charles, his form seemed to stretch out towards Mick as Chrarles ground his teeth together and he let out a yell of his own, pulling back on the light emitting from him, but it seemed to be in vain. Mick seemed to be pulling whatever energy he could from Charles.

Charles fell to a knee and released the staff waving his hand in defeat,chuckling, "I yield, I yield." he smiled up at Mick, "Ya' got me, boyo."

Mick stopped any of his casting immediately and offered the staff to Charles who took it and pushed himself back up to his feet, "I learned from the best, Pops. I thought ya' had me thar fer a second."

"It was a good use of Rigby's Channel, I would'a had ya' otherwise." Charles winked. Then he looked at his staff, a long solid piece of wood covered in decorative etchings. "This took me a long time to make. Really?" he laughed, "You had to pull all of the energy."

"Ya can either win or lose." Mick smiled back, "I made my choice." he let out a hard exhale and threw his hands in the air, launching more sparks and firework-like explosions into the air.

The crowd, who had fallen silent as the two spoke, erupted into cheers and screams of glee as the two shook hands and bowed to each other. A few magical fireworks shot up from the group and the group rushed in to talk to the father and son duo. After a quick embrace, Mick and Charles fell into the group who had engulfed them entirely. For a moment, Mick was on someone's shoulders, but then he was gone in the cheering crowd.

Marcus turned to Di and George in awe, they just stood there smiling.

"How did they do that?" He asked, nearing an accusatory tone. "How can they cast without the Drain?"

George smiled his cheshire grin, "That's what we want to teach you, Marcus. We want to show you that magic, while it still carries a cost, can be cast safely. Follow us."

Chapter Six

Di and George led Marcus over to a red barn next to the farmhous. With how clean the red outside was, Marcus could not tell if it was a new building or not but, from everything that he had gleaned from his brief introduction, he felt safe in assuming that it was maintained by magic. His assumption was quickly confirmed when he walked in through the barn doors with the others.

Inside the barn was significantly larger than the outside, it was packed full of animals, each with their own individual stalls that had some charm on them that made them larger still allowing the animals inside of them to run into endless expanses that somehow joined each other allowing for visits to other pens. Bales of hay flew through the air and into troughs, tools mucked on their own. Horses raced through paddocks while groups as pigs wallowed in mud and ate from troughs ripe with food that fell from orchards three stalls over. Goats climbed mountains, sheep huddled on hills, and the chickens were just clucking and crowing to their heart's content. Marcus grinned a dopey grin. He was never an animal activist, but he had never seen a farm before, let alone live farm animals, and these ones seemed happy, truly happy.

He felt a soft nudge at his lower back and turned around and fell back as he stood face to face with an alpaca in a ski hat. It opened its mouth wide and let out a yell, sending him back further, tripping over the low wall and falling into the mud pits of the pig pens. He fell with a splash and the pigs squealed and scattered from him. He couldn't say for sure but it seemed like the alpaca laughed.

Marcus pushed himself out of the perfectly warmed mud with a sucking sound and cleaned himself off as best as he could which, considering that the mud was made to perfection for the pigs, was not that well. As the alpaca stood there, now clearly smiling at him. Di and George were holding each other up as they were laughing so hard that they couldn't get words out, from the horse stall an airy female voice broke through the laughter.

"You must be this Marcus I've been hearing so much about." The chuckle factory snapped out of it in an instant. "So pleased to meet you."

The voice came from a woman who stepped out of the stall, the shimmer of some invisible wall revealed a portal that the source of the voice phased through. She was a thin, tall, blonde woman with her hair up in a loose ponytail. She smiled a calm grin and adjusted a white knee length tunic that drew attention to her clean bare feet.

"I am," Marcus stammered trying, but entirely unable, to meet her unblinking blue gaze.

"I am Demi," she said with a slight bow, "I have heard great things about you, Marcus."

Marcus returned the bow, he neither had a clear reason in his mind as to why nor the knowledge of how much to bow so he went with a deep nod, and saw that both Di and George had dropped to a knee and bowed their heads. He started to do the same when Demi stopped him.

"Please don't, I hate that they do that." she chuckled, "Traditions are fine and well but the reverence always made me uncomfortable. I see you have met Pach." The alpaca clopped over to her side, "A mischievous one, she is?" She nuzzled the creature scratching at its jaw. She turned back to Marcus, "So is it safe to assume that George and Di have given you the grand tour?"

"Mother," George started "... I mean, Demi." The name came out in a pained, childish tone that didn't suit the George that Marcus knew. "He has only just woke up, we ran into complications."

"The fight with Kallis," she said, nodding, her focus mostly on the affectionate Pach. "Then he is still experiencing the Drain?"

"He is, Demi," Di affirmed.

"Then we are very much behind. Very well then, Marcus." She looked at him, "Do you believe that you are prepared for training?"

Marcus didn't really know what to say. He didn't know what he was training for any better than where he was in space or time. He decided to go with a confident answer. "As ready as I'll ever be." For confident responses, he felt that this was a swing and a miss.

Demi let out a soft laugh, "I guess that is all that we could hope for." her smile literally lit up the room with an unnatural light that left no shadows. She turned to Di and George, "Seriously, three years?"

George stammered something of an excuse but it was entirely too meek as he whispered it into the ground.

"Very well, let's see what you can do." She gestured back towards the pig pen. "Can you make a pig fly? They love it when we do that!" her excitement bolstered Marcus' will.

"I can certainly try!" he said, the words came from a part of him that he hadn't felt before and he already hated whatever part that was. His legs carried him back in through the magic wall and into ankle deep mud, the other three following him out. He looked over his shoulder for a second and George and Di stared, nodding their support, mouths open in uneasy anticipation.

Marcus closed his eyes and focused, feeling out in front of him for the psychic sensation of one of the hogs. He had levitated coins and various small objects before for entertaining friends and clients, but never anything this large. The weight of the pig weighed down on him and he could immediately feel the pressure, as if the pig were sitting on his chest. With a grunt, he heaved one of the average sized pigs into the air a few feet. It squealed with delight and, after a few moments of getting its bearings in the air, started to prance. The movement was just enough to break Marcus' control and it dropped to the ground with a splash. He was exhausted, sweat trickling down his face and the taste of blood in his mouth.

"Again," Demi commanded, her voice no longer supportive.

"I don't think that I can," he said, breathing heavily, looking down at his arms he saw they were starting to bruise a deep purple.

"I don't care if you don't think that you can, you must."

"Did you not hear what I said?" He was angry, this wasn't teaching him anything and he felt the burn of embarrassment turn into the burning of flames as he started to heat up. "I am not your show monkey. I mean, you three, and I only assume you are part of this mess because of how these two seem to give two flying..."

George interrupted, "Marcus! Stop!" his voice carried an air of warning more than anger.

"No, George, you stop! I need answers. Now! In the last twenty four hours, I have lost my girlfriend, had to fight some faceless monsters, I've been kidnapped and taken to Gods know where upstate. Why am I here? You keep telling

Excited to read more about Hugh Glass, they headed for the school library only to find no children's books written about him. Their disappointment over this gave me the desire to write a book for them.

My journey as an author had to wait until I retired from teaching. In preparation for writing, I read "The Song of Hugh Glass" by John Neihardt. This beautifully written epic poem further inspired me to write. Other fictional and biographical books about Glass gave me more insight into his life.

I visited the spot where the grizzly attacked Glass near the forks of the Grand River. I walked the cactus-covered prairie dotted with high buttes and deep ravines. I marveled that Glass had survived such a difficult journey. Several times, I returned there, to the place of the attack. Standing there looking down toward the forks of the river on a late August day, I pictured Glass struggling with the grizzly. Once, two students accompanied me there. We spent several hours roaming the area and imagined we were members of the Ashley Fur Company. We read these words on the monument, situated above the spot where Hugh wrestled the bear:

HUGH GLASS ~ ADVENTURER

Hugh Glass, a member of the Ashley Fur Party under Major Henry, going up the Grand River in August 1823, a habitual "loner", while hunting, was attacked by a grizzly bear near the Forks of Grand River. Horribly mauled, he could not be

moved, a purse was made up, two men, probably
Fitzgerald and Bridger, were left with him and they
probably, believing him dead, took his gun and
accoutrements and left him. He, however, was not
dead and dragged himself to the stream, sustained
himself on seasonal fruit and meat, obtained when
he drove off some gorged wolves from a buffalo
calf they had downed and by some means and by
an uncertain route appeared at Ft. Kiowa, below
the Big Bend, 190 miles as the crow flies from the
Forks of Grand River. That much is verified history.
He was killed by Aricara Indians on the ice of the
Yellowstone River near mouth of the Big Horn in
the winter of 1832-33. John G. Neihart in an epic
poem, "The Song of Hugh Glass" has immortalized
him. Alone, unarmed, terribly wounded it seems
probable he proceeded at night on high ground,
to avoid Indians, sought shelter and water in the
day time and guided by his instinct succeeded in
reaching the Big Bend and Ft. Kiowa. Whatever
the details, it was a marvelous show of stamina
and courage.

After retiring in 2004, I began planning my book. I
decided to begin each chapter in the book with a verse of
Scripture. As I read my Bible each day, I jotted down verses
to accompany the story that was beginning to form in my
mind.

The inscriptions on the Hugh Glass monuments
provided the facts that became the framework of my book.
I wrote my children's book about Hugh Glass based on
those facts. The book is historical fiction, because no one
really knows how Glass survived and reached Ft. Kiowa.

Dani Kling and Conner Palmer behind the
Hugh Glass Monument on the banks of Shadehill
Reservoir a few miles southwest of Lemmon, SD.

On my daily walks, I daydreamed about Hugh Glass. I
tried to imagine what crawling at night through unfamiliar
land would have been like. Knowing that authors should
write about something they have experienced, I thought
about crawling across the prairie some dark night. I couldn't
ever force myself to do that, even in the daytime!

During the summer of 2004, I began writing. I spent
hours at the computer. A few days later, I went back and
completely changed what I had just written. This happened
repeatedly, until I began to doubt that I would ever be able
to complete the book. I had always loved to write. What I
thought would be an enjoyable, simple project became tedious
and worrisome. By the time I completed the manuscript in
2008, I'd rewritten the story over thirty times!

Often, at night a word or idea would come to me. In the morning, I would return to the manuscript and, with the newfound word or idea, be encouraged to continue writing.

I often was called back to school to substitute teach in 2005 and 2006. This was an opportunity to share with the students what I had written. They loved the story and were anxious for me to complete it. Many times when I saw them in the community or at school, they'd ask, "How's your book coming?" Their encouragement and ideas were just what I needed. I probably would have given up on the book if it had not been for their interest.

I began to think about what I would call my book. I knew it was important to choose just the right title. When *Crawl into the Night* finally came to me, I knew it was perfect!

Since I am not an artist, I wondered who would illustrate the book. I made a couple phone calls to people who I thought might be interested. What a relief when Anne Ellingson agreed to be my illustrator! It seemed very appropriate since as a second grader she had once heard me tell the story of Hugh Glass. At that time, she was already interested in drawing.

Gary and I moved from our Prairie City home to our Moreau River Ranch in late 2007. Because of that move, my book was on hold until we were again settled. Since the ranch is rather isolated, it was an ideal spot for concentrating on completing my book.

By May 2008 my book was nearly done. I began to wonder about the next steps...publication and printing. On the advice of an author friend, I researched self-me that I am here to train, to learn. What for? Nothing has been answered. I have been pretty damn cooperative and I have had it just about up to here!" he gestured about three inches above his head. "I mean who the hell are any of you anyway? I trusted you!" He tried to step towards George but his feet were caught in the mud that his heat had dried around his feet and he fell to his knees, his hands sinking into the steaming mud. The pigs were now keeping their distance.

"Well! I'd say, Marcus!" Demi said. "This is a look I haven't seen on you before!" he looked up at her and she was smiling again, with an approving look. "You're right, and that's fair. There is no reason that you would know why you are really here." She shot a glare at George and Di. "You are here because of a battle, more-so a bet."

Marcus interrupted, "Um, excuse me, a bet?"

"I'll only excuse you once, Marcus. Please do not interrupt me again. Like I said, you are here because of a bet. See in the beginning, well..." She laughed, "shoot, I shouldn't even speculate. I guess there was no real beginning except for the old ones, they were what made everything. The plants, animals, and, from all retellings I have heard, through a very circuitous route, eventually humans. Most of us believe that the first humans were dabbling in the desire to be worshiped but it is a rabbit hole that isn't worth diving into right now. Either way, humans came to be and I'll tell you what, you have been nothing but trouble."

"From there, there were... let's call it unintended consequences. As humans worked to explain away every little thing that they could, as much as Gods created humans in their image, humans must have been given a little divinity themselves. Well, they started creating Gods in their image, and you wouldn't believe the monstrosities that are out there." She rolled her eyes and started talking more quickly lost in the idea, "I mean, there are gods with many arms, a flaming crustacean that lives on the opposite side of Jupiter, there is a whole pantheon of what you call the Abrahamic Gods, almost one for each person who believes in them at this point, all arguing over the littlest things. Some that hate their creations, some that think everyone but one small group is going to go to Hell. And don't get me started on the Hells that you people have made up! I mean, the number of bizarre punishment fantasies that involve pineapples have actually resulted in souls being split amongst multiple Hells because it is too hard for a single God to lay claim to the depravity." She shook her head in clear disgust, a look that didn't come naturally to such a beautiful face.

"It all led to a civil war between the Gods, the Earth was a place of terrifying destruction. There were earthquakes and wildfires, hurricanes wiped out coastal cities, leadership was collapsing and people were rioting, killing each other over monetary wealth and which of their Gods was real. It was, well, a complete chaotic failure." she sighed. "You know what I mean?"

Marcus didn't but he nodded.

"Well when it came down to it, the old ones got tired of petty God squabbles and decided to put an end to the unnecessary infighting and took back the divinity of humanity, and they decided enough was enough. They wiped the slate clean. Humans had run rampant, the Gods were killing each other, there were some Gods whose followers had died out ages ago and were literally just making trouble because they were bored, so they did the one thing that made sense. They pulled back their divinity and humanity wiped itself out. This wasn't something any of the Gods wanted, including the Old Ones, so they brought together a council, a pretty even cross section of all of the Gods that had the biggest representation through history and made a plan."

She leaned in and spoke in an excited whisper. "Each of the eighteen lower gods on the council was given the opportunity to choose a champion. Nine Gods were good, nine were... evil sounds a bit diminutive, let's call them chaotic. There were rules, such as the amount of tampering, the number of reincarnations throughout history, that sort of thing, what kind of tips could be given, who could be pushed where. But the idea was that whichever side of the split had a champion who could make it through a series of tests set forth by the council would win control of the world and unbridled privledge over creation. So then we rebuilt the world, brought humanity back, and dropped you in as you always had been, but this time with the Drain, as you call it, and with the Fonts, hoping that giving magic a tangible source would give it a more ceremonial power. We were wrong on that point, but I digress."

"No new Gods would come to be, but the side that succeeded would be given free reign of Earth and, eventually, if the champion of Earth made it through a number of hurdles themselves, one last God, one who would join the council, would be allowed to ascend into God-ship and be a force for whichever side they had represented, there-by tilting the scales in their favor of, and handing control over entirely to, that side. That's where you come in, Marcus. You are the last of your line of reincarnations, you are my champion, the Ra'Saram!"

Marcus wasn't sure how long his mouth had been open, but it was dry. He tried to summon even a single word but found himself a little too nauseous and closed his mouth in hopes that he could keep whatever was coming up in. It was a futile fight and he vomited, purging what little he had in his stomach and not helping with his confusion.

Demi's grin faded a little into disgust, only for a second, "That's new too, hardly the response I was hoping for. But that's fine, I'll take it that you need to gather yourself?"

But he had gathered himself, at least as best he could, enough to ask the only question on his mind, "Why me?"

Demi laughed a booming laugh that shook the barn, "Marcus, you weren't just chosen for this, you were made for this!" She raised her tunic revealing slender pale legs and she showed him a scar on her inner thigh. "I raised you here, before sending you to your birth mother, you were a part of me, the only God touched human to ever be part of this."

"So," Marcus was searching for words, there was too much spinning in his head, "I am here as a pawn in your war?"

"A pawn makes a difference in this war, Marcus. But if we were to break this down to a simple game of chess, I'd say that you were a pawn that made it across the board to become a queen. If that makes you any happier."

It didn't. "So what if I don't want any part of this?" He said. "This isn't something that I asked for."

"Simply put, I cannot force you to be. In fact it has to be your choice. That's one of the rules, but if you choose to not participate, the world will fall to the chaotic Gods," Her face grew somber, "Beings like Kallis will rise to power, find their place as a God, and in all likelihood, humanity will fall again, if not as slaves to their darker overlords, then to the plagues and death that will almost certainly follow."

"Can I think about it?" He asked, not sure what there was to think about but he suddenly understood why Wallace liked to go for a walk if they were fighting. He felt a pain flash in his chest as he thought of Wallace.

Demi must have seen the pain in his face as her tone lightened. "Look, Marcus, we don't have time to think or time to strategize. Kallis is one of the furthest along as far as champions go and is still his first reincarnation, you are the last hope, we have no other champions left and if you back down now, then what happened to Wallace, as unfortunate as it was, will happen to everyone else you know and love, just for fun and because chaos can. Everyone you have ever seen, will die painful deaths. For generations the world will fall under a shroud of suffering. I'm not saying that it would be all your fault, but it is something that only you can stop."

Marcus thought for a moment, he searched his memory for the excitement that he had had at the idea of being able to freely use magic, but didn't find it anywhere, all he felt was dread. He looked at Demi, who, until this point he hadn't allowed it to click in his mind had to be a Goddess of something, and she only offered a smile. George and Di were just as useless for getting any direction, they were still looking at him outwardly mirroring the panic he was struggling to contain. He had never been one for action, not one to work for others. Every part of him fought the idea of laying it all on the line, let alone taking on the responsibility of dealing with a world ending crisis, so he found one thing that would work for him.

"If I do this, would I get to kill Kallis?"

Demi's face softened further, "Him and many others like him."

That was enough for him, for now at least, "Ok then what will I need to do?"

Demi gestured over to the pigs, who had calmed since last having to be part of this ordeal, "Make the damn pig fly, Marcus."

Chapter Seven

Marcus spent the next few hours throwing pigs into the air as best he could. Throwing them was a bit of an overstatement. Much to the chagrin of his three coaches and the pigs themselves, he would have been able to lift them higher by allowing them to stand on his back as he laid in their pen, being only able to levitate them a few feet before dropping them back down into the mud with a solid splash. The pigs, after a few attempts would usually need an emotional break because of the trauma of the drops. That worked in Marcus' favor because he would need a break too. At this point his mouth tasted heavily of blood and his vision was blurred, his arms were almost solid bruise and he was pretty sure that he had torn a lat. He was not progressing.

After some time had passed, Demi would step in and with a wave of her hand wipe the pigs minds of any of the stress that he had caused them, but never offered as much as a helping word to Marcus.

"If I'm supposed to be learning, shouldn't there be someone teaching me?" He finally snapped.

Di stepped forward to caution him but Demi held up a long slender hand. "Marcus, you have everything that you need to be able to do this. Just focus on the other pigs, use them to lift."

Marcus sighed, "That doesn't mean anything to me!" He threw his hands up in the air and plopped down into the mud, the cooling felt good on his sore joints.

"You have to get up, Marcus." Di said, "There is no giving up in this now that you have started."

Marcus didn't feel like he had started anything, everything was a blur, he wanted more than anything at this point just to pass out so that he would get a moment's rest. He pushed himself up and faced the pigs again and, with everything he could give, he let out a yell and lifted it two feet off the ground, another grunt brought it to three, then four. This was the highest he had gotten. Sweat poured now, his shirt would have been see-through had it not been caked in mud. He heaved again and the pig squealed in delight as it flew up another five feet up over his head. For a moment he was happy, but only for a moment as the strength it took to maintain the spell overtook him and he fainted. Just as the world went black, he heard a squeal of terror. He got what he wanted.

He woke up to George standing over him running his hands back and forth over him just as Lance had. Marcus was starting to feel better.

"Here, sip on this, it will make you feel better." Di stood over him offering him a glass of some orange colored juice. "It packs a kick so hang in there."

He took it from her and sucked it down, it wasn't orange juice as he had expected but something with a minty lavender taste, it was not good and he winced as it went down. When he opened his eyes from the grimace, there was nothing but black.

"Guys!" he was panicking, "I can't see!"

"Yeah, well, you were only supposed to sip on it!" Di said. "You idiot! Chugging that down might be permanent!"

"What do I do!?" Marcus yelled around the fingers he had already shoved down the back of his throat, trying to get up whatever he could, apparently either the concoction or his exhaustion had killed his gag reflex.

He felt a cool touch on his wrists pull his hands out of his mouth and George's voice said, "This is supposed to happen," he sounded like he was holding back the kind of laugh that comes out when you are trying to comfort a toddler that hurt itself in a particularly idiotic way. Di was laughing so hard she was snorting. Even Demi let out a chuckle. "This is a potion that we use during training, think of it as an aid to be able to visualize the energy around you. You can still see, just not as you normally do. Calm down and try again."

"You blinded me, for... This isn't worth it. Let the world burn, I'm out." Marcus pushed himself up and he felt his way out of the pen. He walked from pen to pen, feeling his way along the barn wall until he made it to the doors and he stepped out, feeling the sun warm his skin. As he tried to rub his eyes clear of whatever was keeping him from seeing he saw a flash of white. He stood, frozen there for a moment, clinging to the hope that someone would come out after him, just to tell him it would be alright, but as the minutes passed and the blindness remained, he found no comfort, no outstretched hand. In anger he had started pacing and got himself turned around, putting his arms out he tried to find his way back to the barn, but it was in vain. Stumbling along like a fool, he tripped over a root and fell down. Hard.

He laid there, weighed down by his embarrassment. In the dark, all he could do was revisit the past day, the attack by Kallis. He relieved Wallace's death again and again watching her smokey figure choke and sputter before her neck was snapped. For the first time since the attack, he finally allowed himself to cry. A few tears turned to sobs, and the sobs turned to gasping wails as he pounded his fists into the ground. He saw Kallis' face again, smeared with lipstick, smiling back at him. It had all been part of a bigger plan, he had manipulated her, he had pushed himself into Wallace's life to get to Marcus. It had all been a game to cause more pain.

The tears turned back to rage, a comfortable place for Marcus. He found himself calming down and he flipped into a murderous ideation. Rage against the world was his safe place, and now he could expand that anger to the cosmos. Gods, who apparently had been using him for who knows how long, in a game of good versus evil. It wasn't fair, none of this was fair. He had one question on his mind: How could he make them suffer?

More and more he felt the hate flowing through him, he understood, for the first time in a long time, how so many of the downtrodden he had seen on the streets could curse at the heavens as if someone was actually there listening. Maybe they were, but Marcus wasn't going to give them the satisfaction of a word of pain. He pushed himself back up to his knees and closed his eyes in preparation to find his way back to the barn and demand to be taken home. He would face whatever hell was there waiting for him and he was ready for death. This would show whatever playmakers there were that he was still in control.

When he opened his eyes, his vision had changed. He still couldn't see, not in the normal sense. The blackness in front of him lit up with a rainbow of fantastic colors forming a weave of beaded strands of light. To his right a tree, trunk to leaves, was made entirely of a green flowing light coming up from the ground, the grass too, a series of pulsating lights creating a seascape of brilliant illumination. He reached down and touched it and his hands glowed a strong red that, as he touched the grass, calmed to a soft powder blue, the grass taking on a reddish tinge that then faded into the grass around it, as if balancing it out. In that moment, Marcus felt a semblance of peace.

Marcus pushed himself up to his feet, looking around. In the distance he saw people out by the farmhouse, all sorts of colors coming off of them, blues, reds, greens, purples. A full spectrum of energy bouncing between them. He looked up at the sun, only for a moment as it glowed with a full radiant light that filled the sky blinding him. Now able to orient himself, he turned to the barn where three figures stood. George was glowing with a brilliant blue, Di with purple, and Demi, radiating the same full spectrum the sun had. The beauty of it all brought on a calming effect on Marcus and he took a deep breath. When he exhaled, a black smoke, much like that that Kallis' floating head had been made of, flowed from his mouth.

Di extended her arm towards Marcus and a thin wisp of white light started to drift towards him. "Marcus," she said, "we need you. I'm sorry I went about it this way." Her voice was genuine and the wisp started to move around Marcus, a thread of energy wrapping around him.

He started walking back towards the group. It was a futile effort to try and keep an angry face on as he marched back up to them.

"I don't want any more tricks," he demanded.

"We'll do our best," Di nodded, a little blue bursting from her chest. "I mean, maybe a few here and there, but nothing permanent."

"Fine," Marcus did his best to keep a stern face, "Nothing permanent."

Marcus walked back into the barn and was met with another rainbow of colors. The barn's interior glowed with a rich brown, long strands running the length of the charmed building, the entries to the stalls all lit up with a plane of rippling orange, and the stalls themselves shone with a green light.

"What is this?" He asked.

George was the first to answer. "It is the effects of the potion. You wouldn't have lost your sight entirely if you had just sipped it, but since you downed the entire thing, the effects are a bit more severe. The potion is supposed to just let you see the energy around you, the sources that you can draw upon to channel your magic through."

"It's beautiful," he said, poking his head in through the stalls and watching the lights change color as he passed through them and touched them, coursing ripples spreading out around him.

"It is," George continued. "We don't see the colors normally, it is part of the magical effects, but it does let you see the type of magic each charm, creature, and object hold. Everything from the smallest stone to the Sun itself can be channeled." He tossed him a small rock that gave off a stoney blue aura. "Lift this from your hand."

Marcus was relieved to be lifting something smaller than a pig and did so with little effort. He watched as the red light of his palm pushed up and out and lifted the stone like a spindled tower growing beneath it. As he willed it, the spindles started to walk like long spider legs around the stone, spinning it in place. He then floated the stone around his hand and the tendons of light pushed out farther, carrying the stone along with it. Then he floated it around the room, the fibers growing longer and thicker and his hand growing darker as more energy pulled up from his forearm.

"So this is the Drain?" He asked, forgetting that the others could not see what he could.

"Every time you cast," Demi answered, "you have to pull from a source. It could be from a patch of grass, a rock, a river, or a pig."

"But... how?"

"You just have to feel the connection, reach out and you can pull from anything. But all magic comes at a cost still. The Drain is inevitable, but you can choose what to drain. Pull too much and it will kill the source. Pull from something too powerful and it may become overwhelming and the spell can fly out of control. It is the same concept that most people use as focuses. They don't realize that they are channeling so they aren't able to get the full power."

Marcus stepped back into the pig pen and reached out with both hands outstretched. He watched as his red spindles reached out from his fingertips to the glowing red pig. He felt around, concentrating deeply on the pig and for a moment, feeling as though their emotions were shared. His being of determination and the pigs of confusion and apprehension, but they melded into a single thought, "Fly."

With that the pig lifted and Marcus opened his eyes to watch as spindles formed, not only from his hands but from the other pigs, lifting up their floating comrade. Marcus felt the drain but it was less encumbering. He brought the pig higher and reached out to the drift below and felt out for them, taking one hand away from the levitating swine and thrusting it towards the ones below. A few of the spindles from the pigs below that had been supporting the pig above broke and instead connected to him. He felt the power flow into his left hand and through his body into his right and watched as the spindles flowed around him, increasing the light he gave off.

The pig did flips in the air and pranced around happily. It was, for lack of a better term, in hog heaven. Behind him, Marcus heard Di and George whoop and cheer as he brought the pig diving down and launching it in a big loop in the air, he felt a smile crack across his face once again. He was doing it, he was channeling. After a few more minutes, he saw the light begin to dim in the pigs and brought down the flying one safely onto the ground. The drain was minimal but he did still find himself winded and he sat down on a wooden stool inside of the barn.

Both George and Di hurried up to him and clapped him on the shoulder in congratulations as Demi emerged with a large basket of fresh fruit and vegetables that she poured into the green glowing feeding bins outside. The pigs ran over and started eating their bounty and Marcus watched the light returning to them. He wiped the sweat from his brow and his vision returned to normal. He shook his head, something about the vibrance of the world that now seemed artificial.

Demi looked at him approvingly. "Ok now try again, you know what it feels like, try to channel without performance enhancing drugs." She winked.

Marcus closed his eyes and took a deep breath, nodded, and started visualizing the strands of energy and reached out with his hands and opened his eyes. He focused on the biggest pig. It looked into his eyes, ready to go again. As he lifted it up into the air he felt the energy of the other pigs flowing through him. The pig flew upwards, and suddenly he felt the connection waiver, in his sudden loss of concentration, the pig plummeted, landing with a sickening squeal and crunch. It lay motionless, dead on impact.

Demi rushed over to the pig as Marcus collapsed, Di and George running up and trying to get him up out of the dirt. After a few moments of glowing white light from Demi's hands, she turned back to them and shook her head.

"I think we might have expected too much," she sighed. "We will have to push a little harder. Take him to the Loretz.

Chapter Eight

George and Di spun around and started a trek down the hill from the barn towards a small river, maybe fifteen feet across, that ran along the base of the compound. Spanning across it was a weathered wooden bridge crossed the slow, clear water and led to an expanse of fog that blanketed the area beyond it. The bridge, although structurally sound from what Macrus could tell, was out of place in the pristine environment that he had seen so far, giving it an ominous feel like it was caught in the wrong time. The path down was paved with slabs of slate which were still slick with dew but despite that, Marcus flew down after them, lightened by the promise of freedom from the Drain that everyone here seemed to have found.

His mind raced with the potential. A lifetime of conditioning had been shattered by what he had seen but, while the realities of this new world he had found himself in didn't make sense to him, with every step he thought of the wrongs that could be righted, the power he would go back into the world with. The chance to kill Kallis.

George looked over his shoulder from ahead and smiled at Marcus' excitement. It was clear that he had misread Marcus' intentions as he had never condoned violence in the three years that Marcus had known him, but all the same, if there was an energy of positivity in the air and George fed off it.

On the other side of the bridge, a clearing emerged and grew as they made their way down the hill, as if a fog had lifted. The clearing itself was a vast green field of perfectly flat land surrounded on three sides by mountains with plunging cliffs that dove into the river. The only interruption in the sea of grass was a patch of sand that Marcus could barely make out. It was maybe a hundred yards away and only a small, ten foot, square, but it stood out clearly as the only break, its straight lines were unnatural in the rolling serenity.

Di made it to the bridge first and turned to Marcus, her face expressionless "This is the Bridge of Achievement," she said with a hallowed respect, "it is a tool of last resort for us."

George turned once he got to the bridge and continued, "It is a tool used for... quickened instruction, but it is not exactly the most pleasant experience." He let his gaze sink to the ground. "It... well it tends to draw out some pretty dark stuff, Marcus. What we call the Bridge of Achievement is technically called the Loretz, it is a time condensing artifact used in the past to allow the user to achieve something that would otherwise take years. It shortens the passage of time, a day inside of it becoming little more than a second on the outside."

Marcus smiled at them with newfound hope, "This sounds perfect! With you guys helping, I can..."

"We can't go in with you, Marcus." Di cut him off. "This is a one man enters one man leaves kind of thing. You'll be in there yourself, the Loretz itself is more powerful than most of the demi-gods let alone any of us. It keeps you alive for as long as you need to learn, unless what you learn kills you. Marcus, we have never had someone make it through the Loretz's lessons. The last few incarnations of heroes that have gone into this have died inside. They never come out, trapped in whatever pocket dimension this thing makes for them. The fact that you're here can only mean that they died in there."

"Then let's not do it!" Marcus yelled, shrugging and throwing his arms out, submitting to the realization that he was helpless in this. "I have only been at this for a day. I can get better, I swear. It will just take me some time, I mean, if Mick can do it... if those kids up there, I mean, I have to be able to figure it out."

Di looked at him with a look of sullen embarrassment on her face, "Yeah, Marcus, you have to be able to figure it out. The kids have open minds and are able to pick this up quickly, you have years of humanity's negative thoughts and suppositions of magic holding you back. And I mean, let's face it, you're no Mick."

Marcus shook his head in disbelief, "George! Just a few more days. Get me some more of that potion, I was so close!"

George shook his head, still looking at the ground, "We don't have that kind of time, Marcus. If Kallis has made it through the trials of the Gods that we believe that he has, it is only a matter of weeks before he will be able to rise up. Only a matter of days before he kills you. He is more powerful than anyone here, he will find us. It's only a matter of time."

"But what about Demi? She is some sort of God, right?"

Di spoke up, "One of the greatest Goddesses that we have ever met, and she has already interfered too much. It needs to be done this way." She started to cry, hiding her face as best she could by looking at the ground. "If there was any other option..." she trailed off and Marcus knew that there wasn't a better option, not on that timeline, he could feel the weakness from the Drain lingering in him and that only magnified his self doubt.

He took a deep breath, "Fine, whatever," he smiled and tried to feign comfort with what was happening. "So what do I need to do?" If this was going to be the way that he died, he might as well go in having read the instruction manual.

George put his hand on the bridge, "Marcus, Kallis is nearly two thousand years old, he has killed you hundreds of times. If you do this, you have to be one hundred percent sure that you want to do this and commit yourself wholeheartedly or the bridge will not accept you."

Marcus felt George's words hit him and thought about what he was really risking. He couldn't go back to his life, he was a fugitive. The woman that he was about to propose to was now almost certainly dead. His life was over, this was an opportunity to die in a better way than he was likely to if he chanced it out in the world alone.

"George, as far as I'm concerned, I died yesterday. Everything I love is gone. The world that I knew then is gone, I'm operating on a new set of rules. If I am going to die in there, so be it. If I make it to the other side and can kill Kallis, even better. I don't want this life, but it is the only one, heck, the last one I have! Am I right? Might as well go deep." He cracked a smile that felt twisted and out for place on his face, none of that had been true but he had always wanted to give a heroic speech and saw a chance. As far as he could tell, it seemed to lift their spirits a little.

"Ok," George looked up at him for the first time since they started explaining, Marcus could see that his eyes were puffy and his face streaked with tear marks. "You just have to walk onto the bridge and let it know what you want to learn. It will decide how to best do that based on your words, but make sure that you are specific, otherwise you can end up stuck in an unwinnable scenario."

Marcus took a few steps forward and made his way up to the bridge, pausing for a moment to look at Di and George, they gave him nods and he stepped onto the first wooden plank. Nothing happened.

"This is a bit anticlimactic," he scoffed, still making

attempts at bravery. Di let out a snotty chuckle and nodded.

As he reached the peak of the bridge he turned back again, realizing that he wasn't entirely sure of what he wanted to learn, but as he opened his mouth to ask, there was a sudden thunderous cacophony of sound that came from the mountains surrounding them, Marcus took two steps back, moving further down the bridge, and snapped his head side to side, facing the source of the sound just in time to see a wall of water, twenty feet tall, rushing towards him on both sides. He ran down the other side of the bridge to the grass as the wall smashed together behind him.

The water held for a moment, moving like a waterfall in an endless loop of raw natural power. Marcus watched as the water continued to spin and churn in the air, slowing down. With the sound of a loud, single chime it froze into a sharp ice structure that blocked him in, and his view, to the other side of the river. It spanned the entire length of the river, from cliff to cliff and the semi-transparent interior shone with a mixture of blue, green, and purple light that danced around playfully in the light. For a moment it rang with a single tone, and then silence.

Marcus couldn't hear anything around him. There were no birds, no wind, the sound of the river had even disappeared. As he took a few steps on the grass, even his footfall was muffled. He tried yelling out but the sound that came out was like he was underwater. He looked around, trying to find any indication of what to do next and silently made a promise that he would make sure to ask more questions before getting into any more magical mysteries, but now he would have to deal with this one on his own.

Then, from the silence a booming voice filled his mind, "What is it you seek?" It was a strong male voice that carried a presence that made Marcus shake. It wasn't malicious but it was more powerful than anything he had ever felt even if it was only a voice.

"I'm not entirely sure," Marcus said, "I am supposed to be here to learn."

"And what is it that you are here to learn?" The voice in his head boomed again.

"I am supposed to be some kind of a hero, I don't know." For a moment there was more silence, it was just long enough for Marcus to find what he wanted. "I want to learn everything I need to know to kill Kallis."

The sky blackened and the ground shook. The sun disappeared, leaving a sliver of the moon and the stars above him and Marcus was cast into a nearly blinding darkness.

"Then you will fill this valley with corn." The voice told him, now calm. The ground fissured in front of him and the sand pit from the center began to bubble like boiling water, pouring out to cover the entire area. Marcus took a few steps back as it approached him and was able to stay on top of it. In the center of the valley was now a series of dozens of burlap sacks, each with a single word: Corn.

"What the heck am I supposed to do with this?" Marcus yelled, pointing at the ground around him, "You can't grow in sand!" but there was no answer. Then again, why would there be? He was entirely alone.

He walked over to the stacks of seed and pushed them around a little bit to see if there was anything else printed on the bags, possibly instructions. No luck. The bags were large and heavy and way too difficult to carry around. There were no tools, no water, just seeds. He sat down against them to think. Looking around, there were nearly ten acres of sand that had covered the dirt.

"Of course!" he yelled and started digging to get down below the sand. After a few feet he resigned to the reality that there was nothing under the sand, just more sand. "Of course not," he shook his head. The whole place was magic, some kind of puzzle that he would have to solve. His stomach grumbled and he realized it had been a long time since he had eaten. He thought back to what George had said, that the Loretz enchantment would keep him alive, as long as what he was studying didn't kill him first. He figured a meal of some kind would magically show up and once he had eaten, he would be able to think more clearly.

So he sat and waited, and waited, and waited, minutes bleeding into hours as nothing came and the hunger continued to grow. He reached into the sack of corn and took a few dried kernels and popped them into his mouth, allowing them to soak until he could crunch them down and eat them. It was gross, but it was something. When no meal showed up he realized he was in trouble. If he had to worry about hunger, he would probably have to worry about thirst and with the river being frozen, the magical ice didn't seem like it would offer any aid. He ran over just to make sure and was unable to break anything off it.

From the wall he looked out at the valley, treeless and filled with sand. That dawned on him too. In any movies that he had seen where there was sand, it got hot, and he didn't have any shade either. The next few hours he dedicated himself to moving around the corn bags so that he could safely dig out a hole to act as shade that he could climb down into and hide from whatever blazing heat there was to come.

Once that was done, he sat back up against the bags of seed and tumbled a few kernels around in his hand, sticking one into the ground for good measure. "There you go!" he reassured himself, "One down, a hundred million more to go, no biggie!" he looked around at the daunting task that lay ahead of him. He wasn't ready, no part of him could move with the weight of the situation building around him. The more that he looked around the heavier it all got, until between the hunger and the panic, he fell asleep.

Chapter Nine

When Marcus woke up it was still dark, the moon was still a sliver overhead and the stars still mocked him from above as if they were counting out how many more seeds he had to plant. Marcus grabbed a few more dry kernels and moved them around in his mouth, trying to build up the saliva to melt them down to a chewable consistency but couldn't summon the spit. His mouth was dry and he choked a little as he swallowed them down. Again, it wasn't much but his stomach seemed to appreciate even the littlest bit of sustenance that he provided. He managed to force down a few more but knew they wouldn't sustain him.

"What are you trying to prove?" He yelled at the moon, which for him was enough of a figure in the sky to be blamed for what was happening. Then it clicked, it had to be proving that the effort was futile, that him learning what he needed to know to beat Kallis was as much a wasted effort as planting seeds in sand. He was going to be trapped in here until he starved because he had chosen the wrong words. He sank down into the sand, leaning against the bags of corn, and wept, openly, into his hands ready to accept his fate.

He started to feel the all too familiar feeling of hate growing inside of him. He hated that he was stuck in here, he hated the Gods for forcing him into a war that he wasn't even sure of what side he was actually on, he hated Di and George for having tricked him like this. Then an idea crossed his mind.

This had to be a trick of Kallis' to trap him and keep him in place until he could kill him himself. He leapt up to his feet and looked around for any sign of the legions soldiers he was sure would pop up any moment now. There were none. Again, even his imaginary enemies weren't there, he was alone. He kicked at the sand. Damn how he hated that sand. His foot sank into the imprint that he left and the grainy warmth wrapped around it as the rim of the impact sank back into the hole.

"The sand!" he looked up and around, nothing had changed, but he started to think of what he had learned in the barn, everything had some power, pigs, trees, grass, even a pebble. Maybe even the sand had some power. He closed his eyes and focused, putting his hand into the sand. He felt the warmth and the coarse sand gritting against his hand and sure enough, he felt something else, an energy stored in the sand itself. Urging the strength that he could from it, he was able to find the seed that he had pushed into the ground just by reaching for it with his mind.

"Grow," he said out loud, commanding the seed. He felt the power from the sand run through him and out his outstretched hand. The sand went cool around him and when he opened his eyes a small sprout had sprung up. It was barely a blade of grass itself, but it was something.

Marcus jumped up and whooped triumphantly, throwing his fists in the air and pointing at the moon laughing at it mockingly. He danced around that little sprout like he had won the lottery. Over the next hour he moved from spot of sand to spot of sand channeling what power he could pull from it and pushing it into the growth of a fully formed stalk, ear and all.

A clap broke out from behind him, "Ya did a good job there, boyo!" It was Mick.

"Mick! What are you doing here?" Marcus yelled over to him, "I figured it out, man! I figured out how to channel!"

"Good job, Marcus!" he smiled, "I am only here ta' give ya' some water," he said, holding out a canteen in one hand, "and a little drink yer'self if ya'd like it?" he wiggled a flask in front of him in the other.

"The bridge let you in here?" Marcus asked, seeing that the ice wall was still intact. He took the canteen and chugged a few glugs out of it.

"Careful there, bud, don' wanna finish that off too quick. Last freebie you'll git fer a while."

Marcus nodded and screwed the lid back on and put the water into his shade hole.

"Well! Good luck, Marcus!" Mick waved and with a loud pop disappeared.

Marcus looked back at his cornstalk with pride and reached out and grabbed the corn and snapped it from the stalk. The bulging kernels drew him in and he took a bite. It was more than he had ever dreamed it could be. The ear burst with sweet flavor and, most importantly, juice. He ate his way down the ear like a cartoon character, flying through row after row until it was picked clean.

"Alright," he put his hands on his hips and looked around, "now to just make the rest of the field." It took him several hours to move from spot to spot in the sand to gather up enough power to grow a few more plants. In the end he had spent over eight hours of backbreaking work to grow up thirty-five plants, it was barely enough to even make a dent in the field. After the last plant had formed and Marcus couldn't find anymore of the energy in the sand to channel, he looked up, half expecting to have his view obstructed by the forest around him. His heart fell when he saw that there was only a scattering of plants. He paused and looked around, the light dusting of crops making the scale of the sand seem even more vast and that vastness made him feel like he had even more work to do and now that he had sucked up all of the energy from the sand, there would be no way to do it.

He sat down with another ear of corn and made it about halfway through before he fell asleep, kernels in his mouth and a half eaten ear in his hand, the physical exhaustion getting the best of him.

When he woke up, Marcus was face to face with Di. She was crouched over him close enough that it was the feeling of her breath that woke him.

"You're still in here?" She chuckled, "I could have gotten this done in a few hours."

"So why don't you show me how to do this?" He asked, pushing himself up to his feet looking around to see what had changed to let Di in. The ice was still in place and the sky was still dark. From what he could tell there had been no change.

"You know I couldn't help even if I wanted to, Marcus. This is your task." she said a little too matter of factly. "I am not positive of what happens, but from everything I've been told, the Loretz would kill me if I even tried."

"So then what are you even doing here." He growled.

"Heck if I know. One second I'm out teaching kids how to float pumpkins, next I'm here." She shrugged. "Magic am I right?"

"Ok, well if you can't help then you are just getting in my way. I am stuck in this permanent darkness, apparently." He gestured out to everything around him, not pointing at anything in particular but still appropriately identifying the source of his frustration, "I've got work to do." He pushed past her and grabbed a handful of seeds. In his sleep he had dreamt up the idea of channeling the other stalks to grow another one. At least that is what he had gotten from the dream, which involved a banker repeatedly telling him to focus on continuous growth and compounding interest but he figured that had to be related to the task at hand.

He scooped up some more sand and put a seed in, covering it back up and focusing on the energy that the other nearby stalks had to offer him. He heard a snort from behind him.

"What?" He snapped.

"Nothing," Di said defensively, "it just looks like you are trying really hard at this, if only you had something like magic to make that process easier. It's just that you look like a baby horse learning to walk on ice. You're all magical legs, man."

He stiffened and felt rage growing inside of him. Where he knelt turned slick and it cracked. Looking down, the sand below him turned to glass and cracked, the thin spidery lines filling with little rivers of blood. He took a second and a few more calming breaths.

"I... am... just... trying... to... get... through... this..." he panted, the breaths not helping with the sharp pain in his knee as his body bobbed.

He saw a twinge of surprise that may have been fear flickering across Di's face, "It's okay Golden Boy," she smiled a forced grin, "I'm sure you'll figure it out. You should probably start by not killing off your plants!" and with a look of disappointment and a loud pop, she too disappeared.

Marcus stood up and brushed off his knee, pulling out

the little spines of glass that were stuck in it. The warm blood trickled down his leg, it looked black in the darkness and reflected the stars in a pretty little stream. Looking up at the stalks around him, he realized that they had become black and wilted as he had pulled all the energy out of them, as Di had said, killing them.

Marcus let out a loud groan and roared a throat ripping yell. Nearly a day's work had gone into those plants and there was not enough energy left in the sand to make any more. He wasn't just back at step one, he was set back before that. He wracked his brain for an option. He tried channeling the kernels themselves, only to find that they too turned to rot instantly if he channeled them, he tried with the stalks that were left, but they wilted too, he was unable to make so much as another sprout from the energy left in the Loretz, he was dead in the water.

With another yell he summoned all of the energy that he had and pulled from inside himself focusing everything that he had into the kernel he had planted. A little stalk wriggled out of the ground just as he passed out from the Drain.

The next few days, or at least what he was pretty sure were days as he had lost track of time because the moon never moved, were spent the same way. He would bury a seed and then cast from himself to have it grow a small stalk. He would pass out and then wake up and do it again. The plan slowly took shape that he would grow all of the small stalks that he could and let them grow on their own until there were enough that he could channel them safely. He continued to eat the dry kernels, now having developed a taste for them.

Routinely passing out from the Drain was beginning to wear on him. He was now losing clumps of hair and had regular nosebleeds that he hadn't even tried to blot away at this point. His shirt was stained with blood and the pricks in his knee from the glass never seemed to heal, his pant leg from the knee down now soaked through with his blood. He knew that he couldn't keep this up and that if he did he would die within a week but he pressed on. He was able to pass out and wake up every few hours and, if his estimates were correct, he would be able to plant a small patch that he could channel in ten days time.

By the fifth day he wasn't able to stand anymore. He was completely sapped, with only enough energy to suck on a handful of kernels with no spit to soak them in let alone swallow.

After a week he wasn't able to move. He just lay there, looking at the stars, ready for whatever death awaited him.

"What a way to go," he let out a raspy chuckle, "I don't even get my big fight, just this damn corn." He laughed a full belly laugh and it hurt, "It's not much, but it's honest work." He summoned enough energy to take a prone swing at the nearest bag that he had been eating from. The impact hurt him more than it hurt the bag.

Then he heard a voice at his feet, a voice that sent chills down his spine. "Maybe I can help you with that, Ra'Saram."

Marcus swung his head as best as he could to see the origin of the voice. Standing over him with a grin that exposed a perfect row of teeth filed to points, was Kallis. He towered over him, his hair long and black and it moved in an non-existent breeze, contrasting with his pure white three piece suit. Had he not come with the intent of murder, he would have been a funny sight to behold.

"It has been far too long, Marcus." Kallis said as if greeting an old friend. "Looks like I found you at a bad time." He looked around at the sky, "A Loretz, eh? Thought you would be able to get a leg up?"

It took all of his energy but Marcus pushed himself up to his good knee, it was the tallest that he had the power to make himself and the farthest he had been from the ground in days. The effort made him dizzy.

"Kallis, you can't hurt me here. The enchantment..."

"Is childsplay!" Kallis roared. He waved his hands and sent the bags flying. "It was only a matter of time before I found you, you must have known that. A little time warp spell isn't going to change that. These are the playthings of lesser Gods, a power that I surpassed eons ago." he laughed.

Marcus struggled to get to his feet but crumpled again, landing on his knees and he let out a yell as a pain shot through his body.

Kallis took a few steps closer, so that he loomed over Marcus, blocking out the moon. "Now let's have a little bit of fun before I end this. What do you say?"

Marcus opened his mouth to respond but Kallis swept his arms in front of him and skin formed over Marcus' mouth, sealing it shut.

"I don't think I need any interruptions, I have a bit of a monologue prepared, showmanship is such a lost art amongst the Gods, I plan to bring that back. Now where was I? Ah, yes." He flapped his arms up and down as if he were trying to take off, faster and faster until they began to blur together. Marcus watched in horror as they slowed and he was able to focus on them. Instead of two arms, Kallis now had eight arms that each moved independently of each other. Two of the arms stretched out towards Marcus, elongating freely like eldritch tentacles, and wrapped around his chest and arms in a tight grip that squeezed the breath out of him. Marcus struggled against the squeeze but between the exhaustion and their raw strength, he couldn't budge.

"Good, now that I have your attention, let's put on a little show." Kallis waved his two of his free arms and in front of Marcus, Wallace appeared, this time without all of the smoke. There, sitting in front of him in full color, bound and gagged in a chair, was Wallace. She was bruised all over, bleeding from her eyebrow and nose, and eyes red and swollen from crying. Marcus let out a yell for her but it was muffled by the seal over his mouth.

"Marcuf," Wallace cried, "I'm tho thorry." she was sobbing and he could barely make out the words through the cloth gag, but she yelled around it.

"Ugh! What a horrible sound!" and with a snap Kallis made the gag disappear. "There we go, cry your heart out, girl!"

"Marcus, I swear I didn't know. I didn't know what I was doing, he was controlling me! You know I'm not that person! I swear I'm not! Please, Marcus. Forgive me! There was some sort of enchantment on me, you know I love you!"

Kallis overacted a gagging sound and snapped his fingers, sealing her mouth as well. "See Marcus, she is still alive, I lied to you before. I felt that a little leverage would be perfectly fine to have moving forward. Marcus, Wallace is alive and, for now, unharmed enough that she will likely be able to survive her wounds. So whaddya say we strike a deal?" His arms gave him a little squeeze to accentuate the point.

Marcus started to speak but again was blocked by the skin over his mouth.

Kallis laughed a big hearty laugh, "Of course! I knew I was forgetting something, this was just so damn exciting! Look at you, I want to negotiate for your beloved's life and I have left you voiceless. Silly me! You know how you get so into something after so much rehearsing that you forget something so basic that it breaks the flow?" He shook his head and rolled his eyes, slapping one of his hands against his thigh. He snapped his fingers and the skin ripped, painfully. "There we go! So whaddya say? Your life for hers? No no no, we have tried that before, I want to put a real end to this, how about where you are for her life? I want to deal with this ranch of yours once and for all."

Marcus gasped as he readjusted to having a mouth. After wiggling his jaw a bit, he said, through the dry interior, "Can... can I... have a drink? I am terribly parched."

Kallis smirked, feigning amusement, "An interesting choice for a last meal. If you agree and share where you are, I would be happy to indulge."

Marcus cracked a smile, splitting his lip enough that he could feel the blood bead and run down into his mouth, "I think now would be best, see I am just so damn thirsty and I think it would be hard for me to negotiate with such a dry mouth." Once again he was not a fan of whatever this bravery was.

"Well I am sure I can swing something," Kallis' smile grew wider and he lifted a hand and made a motion like he was squeezing an orange. Wallace let out a muffled scream as she writhed in agony and a red mist burst from her. "I hear a little sip of love will wet your whistle for living." He pulled a crystal chalice from his jacket and the mist pooled in the air and poured itself into the cup. Kallis swirled it around and gave it a sniff, "Ahh like a fine wine, go ahead, Marcus." He reached the cup towards Marcus, "This is the perfect vintage for a good negotiation. Drink her in."

He poured the drink against Marcus' pursed lips but a little got through and Marcus could taste the warm blood in his mouth. Marcus spat and sputtered as Kallis laughed so hard he dropped the glass chalice and it shattered in the sand.

Kallis stopped laughing and looked down at the ground. "Yikes, now that is a hazard! Have you ever tried to clean glass out of sand? It is a real pain, I'll tell you what. Here, would you mind cleaning that up for me?" and he thrust Marcus down against the sand and Marcus' knees buckled and he fell, kneeling down into the glass. "I think I prefer you kneeling in front of me, anyway."

Marcus grimaced as the glass cut into his legs, but unable to stop himself he chuckled, "Phrasing."

Kallis gave him a twist, wringing his back like a towel, and Marcus screamed as more glass ground deeply into his knees, "Well, Marcus, it seems you have your voice back." His voice was more of a growl than it had been before "I have made a bit of a change to what I need from you though, you have wasted my time beyond what I actually was hoping to spend with you. What do you say I give Wallace a quick death and you a slow one?" he paused for a moment and stretched out the offer as if he were making it up as he went. "If you are willing to give up your location."

Marcus spat blood that speckled Kallis' suite with small red dots, "I don't think that's going to work for me, see, I want a pizza, three armored vehicles, a police escort to the airport and a plane to take me wherever I want to go loaded with one hundred thousand dollars worth of green gummy bears." He couldn't stop, every alarm in his head was going off, he was screaming at himself inside to shut up but he was positive that the Wallace that he was seeing now was something else, just an illusion that Kallis had made to convince him and that, for some reason, made him mad enough to run his mouth. In his best Russian accent he added, "and diplomatic immunity."

"That's cute," Kallis was no longer trying to hide his boredom with the conversation. "You think she isn't really Wallace?" Marcus' smile fell off his face. "That's right, I can read your mind. I mean, by the Gods, what part of magic don't you understand? Let me go ahead and prove it to you.

Let's see what it takes."

With another snap of his fingers, Wallace's mouth reappeared and her bindings fell off her.

"Go ahead, dear, run to him."

"Marcus!" She yelled running towards him. Marcus saw it in her eyes, there was a certain spark, it was really her, he didn't doubt it anymore. She only made it a few steps before Kallis stretched out one of his arms in an arching swipe and Wallace dropped, her head at an unnatural angle. She was dead in the sand.

Marcus let out a sob and looked into her eyes, they were filled with horror, a twisted scream stuck silently on her face.

"You know what's interesting, Marcus? The guys that I bat for, they give me real power, none of that granola crunching garbage you are shovel fed. I have killed you and your ilk thousands of times now. Just, over and over again an endless history of failures. Not a single guy on my team has gone down yet. Not once, not ever! Good never triumphs. You know why?" He leaned in close and whispered, like he was sharing a secret, "Because Chaos is the master of life and death. We are eternal and we will always win."

Kallis leaned in conspiratorially, his lips touching Marcus' cheek "You aren't willing to do what is necessary to live, to win. You can't do what a God can do because you cannot fathom being a God. I can because I am. Watch." With four of his hands he reached down to Wallace and coaxed strands of white, blue, and green light into her from his undulating hands.

Her head twisted back into place with a sickening crunch and, after a moment, she gasped back to life, screaming.

"Marcus, stop him!" she managed to beg between gasps as the color came back to her face.

Kallis grabbed her and threw her back a few feet where she landed on the ground panting. "Oh good, this is fun, isn't it, Wallace? Looks like she might have gone to the bad place this time. Yikes! She and I have been doing this all day as I was trying to find out what she knows. You know, she has been very useful. Such a shame to hear about your childhood, I would have hoped that your last life would at least be something you enjoyed. It isn't as much fun taking something that isn't wanted in the first place. You know what I mean?"

Marcus had nothing to say, he was just watching Wallace to see if she got back up, staggering uneasily to her feet.

Kallis took the silence as an invitation to continue, "I mean look at you, killing you now is like winning the lottery by taking a set of old broken tires from a homeless man who doesn't have a car. Like what are you even doing with your life that you continue to cling to it? I mean, I get it, 'I want to live' is a great message, but after everything that has happened to you, is it even worth it? Why bother continuing the struggle? It's ok to welcome death, Marcus." He paused and thought for a second, "You know what? Don't answer, I don't care. I'm just happy to put you out of your, and more importantly my, misery."

He raised all six of his free arms and started moving his fingers in intricate formations, mumbling under his breath as each hand glowed with a different color ball of light. Blue energy crackled, green lights flicked around emitting golden sparks, red light seemed to bubble and pop, purple swirled in a shining whirlpool, yellow light radiating a great warmth, and orange light let out a quiet humming sound as it pulsated and grew.

"Good bye, again, for the last time, Marcus." He drew his hands back and brought them forward, Marcus winced and looked away and heard Kallis let out an "Oof" just before there was a loud bang.

Marcus looked back to Kallis, between them in a smoking heap, was Wallace, she had run and thrown herself into Kallis throwing him off for a second and it looks like she took the brunt of the spell. She laid there motionless, her clothes smoking from the spells hitting her. Her eyes were wide open, looking at Marcus a smile plastered on her still face. She was dead but she had stopped Kallis, at least for a second.

Kallis righted himself again having only stumbled from the impact. He looked down at Wallace's body and shook his head, "No no no, this won't do." He put his hands back on her and the burning stopped, a moment later she was back to life gasping for air.

"Stop it!" Marcus yelled thrashing as best he could against Kallis' grip but it was still too strong to break.

"I'm trying to, but she keeps ruining my moment, Marcus." Kallis snapped back with a twinge of humor in his voice, "If we could just get through this I can be done, she can be dead, you'll be dead, I'll be a God. I can just relax!" He took a second to gather himself as Wallace pushed herself up to her feet, once again squaring off against him. He snapped his fingers and her leg made a sickening cracking sound as her knee bent backwards and she screamed, her femur shooting out of her thigh a few inches and her face draining of color. Her eyes rolled back in her head as she started to lose consciousness from the pain.

"Please, Kallis, let her go! Please I'll do anything!" Marcus pleaded, his face now streaming with tears as he watched Wallace struggle up to her one good leg.

"Anything?" Kallis grinned, "Tell me where you are."

"Don't tell him, Marcus." Wallace yelled.

"Where are you?" Kallis yelled again.

"I can take him, don't tell him anything!" Wallace yelled again.

Kallis looked at her as if she had just told him that the sky was made of birthday cake. "You can what?" he scoffed, snapping his fingers again, her good leg snapping backwards as she wailed and fell to the ground again.

"Stop hurting her, please. Her life for mine and where we are." Marcus tried to fall back on an earlier deal.

"Hmmm..." Kallis put a finger to his chin, "I don't think

that was the deal, clocks ticking loverboy, want to sweeten the pot?" He rolled his wrists and snapped his fingers and Marcus watched as two ribs cracked and shot through the back of Wallace's bloodstained shirt. She screamed and grabbed her stomach.

"Fine, fine, just give her a quick death. I'll give you what you want." Marcus begged looking up at Kallis. He didn't know where they were but he knew the general location, that would have to be enough.

"I'm afraid renegotiation counts as a refusal of terms and the offer is now no longer in effect, Marcus. You'll have to do better now." He smiled and again two more ribs cracked out of Wallace.

Marcus scrambled for anything that he could think of to offer, he had nothing, he was ready to betray anyone it took, he would work for Kallis, he was ready to die to just have this over, anything to stop being forced to watch as Wallace bled out on the ground, her life flowing out of her, anything to get off this glass. Then he paused.

"Wait, wait, I have an offer." He took a deep breath and closed his eyes, if he was going to try this he would only have a second so he was buying whatever time he could afford.

With one more deep breath he reached out in his mind to feel for Wallace's life force, he reached in and did his best to siphon the energy into him. With a strong exhale he sent a gale force of wind at Kallis sending sand into his eyes. Instinctively, Kallis let him go and grabbed at his eyes rubbing them to get the grains out. That was the moment that Marcus needed.

"I'm sorry Wallace," he yelled, "I forgive you." He channeled everything that he could from her as he brought the sand shooting up from every side of Kallis at every angle that he could. With a stomp and a scream, Marcus pushed out every bit of heat that he could, instantly turning the sandstorm into a tornado of glass. It sliced and shredded at Kalls as the shards got larger in both size and number. With one final push, Marcus sent them all inwards towards him, impaling him with thousands of blades of glass.

Kallis looked at him with a confused look on his face, "But I..." and he fell over with a squishing sound as the glass pushed deeper into him. He was dead.

Marcus did his best to fall towards Wallace's lifeless body. He sobbed as he lifted her head and cradled it in his lap. "We won, Wallace, we did it." he sobbed.

As he bent down to kiss her, Wallace started to disappear. She sank through his hands and evaporated into a cloud of smoke as her ghostly form hit the ground. Marcus looked around in confusion, around him the scene was changing. Kallis' body had done the same thing, leaving a pile of glass on the ground where he had laid, the sky turned to daytime as the sun burnt through the shroud of night, and the ice wall began to melt away revealing the other side of the bridge where George and Di stood, exactly in the same place that they had been when he entered.

Marcus looked around him, the bags of kernels were gone, the sand had receded into its original pit. On the other side of the bridge, Di and George were now cheering and calling him to come to them but he didn't have the energy, he just fell back into the grass and laid there, looking up at the sky. The sound of the river came back to him, birds chirped in the trees, and a warm breeze swept over him. Alone and safe in this field, he wept.

Chapter Ten

The next few days were a blur for Marcus. Once he finally left the field, it took him a long time to be convinced that what he had seen wasn't real and that it had all been a test created by the Loretz to get him through his training. Both Di and Mick swore up and down that they hadn't been in there, Di even insisted that it hadn't even seemed like any time had passed at all. She and George hadn't had enough time to even finish a conversation at the bridge before it was all over. Finally, after some convincing Marcus came to terms with the reality that the fight was only just beginning and that the projection of Wallace that he saw was only a manifestation of the subconscious that the Loretz had been able to pull from him.

She was never there. She was still dead.

It wasn't until the third morning of wallowing in the bedroom that George had put him in that Marcus was able to get out of bed and continue his training. Up to that point everyone had respected his need for time and space. After hearing his story, everyone who saw him the first few days avoided making eye contact for too long and only visited the room they had made up for him to offer him fresh meals and freshly pressed fruit drinks. He turned it all away. That third morning though, Di called an audible on George's plan to let him heal on his own.

After another evening that Marcus had been unable to sleep through, she burst into his room right as the sun started to rise.

"OK! I think this has been enough healing. If the Loretz let you out, it means you are ready to go, let's see what you can do." She brought with her a breakfast tray, a cup of coffee and a few brownies that Marcus immediately recognized as George's. Judging by the smell they were fresh which meant that George had been up to make them.

Di tossed the tray down onto his bed, "He has been up every morning making these in hopes that you would come down. Biggest meals that I have ever seen him cook, all wasted since the princess won't come down from her tower."

"Look, Di, I really want to do this for you, I just need some time to pick myself back up."

"No time to sit around, Marcus!" she pushed back,

"The enemy is at our gates, the dragon is leading the charge, and our white knight is still in his dressing gown! Get up, some sun will do you good!"

"Gee, thanks, I'm cured," Marcus rolled over and pulled the sheets over his head. He heard the crash of the plate falling and breaking on the floor followed by hurried footsteps running upstairs to his door.

From beneath the covers, he heard George's voice, "Di? What did I tell you about bothering... oh... that was my mother's dish." Marcus could hear the disappointment in his voice and he pulled the comforter down and looked out.

"I'm sorry, George," he said, looking down and the shards of plate scattered in a pile of brownies. He reached to his bedside and grabbed a bouquet of flowers that someone had left him. Focusing on them, he was able to draw enough power to pull the pieces up into the air and put them all back together, the flowers wilting and dying in his hand.

"It's not a problem, Marcus." George said, "Just a sad way to treat someone else's memories and hard work is all." He took the plate from the air and started picking up the brownies off the floor as Marcus watched him, guilt filling his heart. He got out of bed and helped clean up. He was only in his boxers but in this moment, his near nudity wasn't a point of embarrassment, being a victim to his mood was.

"Sorry, George." He said earnestly, "I didn't mean anything by it. I'm just in a rut, you know how it is, man."

"I get it, Marcus, but as you're sitting here everyone is wondering what is going on. I've been telling them that you are tired from the Loretz but you are the first to actually make it out, everyone planned a celebration that, at this point, has fallen pretty flat without the guest of honor."

Marcus felt a twinge of excitement hit him as he envisioned a celebration in his honor. When he and Wallace were together he had done a few birthdays with the guys from Sal's but he had never really been celebrated, those had been excuses for the guys to drink. The moment the thought entered his mind he instinctively pushed it out. He didn't feel like a homecoming hero, he didn't even feel like himself anymore and the person he felt like didn't deserve celebration. Watching Wallace die again and again only to be killed at his hand had taken it out of him. He sat back down in the bed and looked at the grease marks left on the ground and his mind turned them to blood, shifting from brown-beige smudges into pools of red blood and back. He blinked and they stayed as grease.

"None of that, now," Di said seeing his face rise and fall. "It's time to get you up and out. Up and out I say!" She grabbed him by the arm and pulled him from the bed, he ached from not moving and had been happy where he was, but for once saw the potential to be part of something more, he felt the community beckoning him and he couldn't help but oblige, if not out of guilt, out of self preservation, Di's grip, once again, pulling his arm in ways that it shouldn't move.

With a groan he made his way up and out of the bedroom, taking a second to put on the clothes that George had given him. As they started walking down the stairs to the first floor, Marcus paused, the other two stopping with him.

"So, I mean, what's next?" He had no idea what was in store and, if the Loretz had taught him what he needed to know, he had a lingering fear that had developed over the last few days that he would have to face him again. He felt a pang of guilt, his time in the Loretz had felt so real that he felt the lingering presence of having both watched Wallace die, again and again, and having killed her himself. What was worse than that was that he felt something else, he thought it was a sense of peace with what he had done, but it was wrapped in a trench coat of agonizing loss. Maybe that was what peace felt like? He wasn't sure.

George looked up at him from a few steps down, "More training. While the Loretz found its own way to teach you what you needed to know to defeat Kallis, I, all respect to the process, feel that it will not, nor will it ever, be enough." He shook his head and pursed his lips thinking for another moment. "We need you to learn how to stop other casters from channeling your life force. That's our next step. It was what you did to..." he stopped, realizing where he was going, and pivoted. "If you are channeled by another caster, they can kill you without ever casting a spell. They can essentially absorb your life force and you will die. So we have worked out a way to resist that." He started back down the stairs, talking away from Marcus, "Funny story actually, I discovered this technique about two hundred years ago when I was talking to a catfish."

"Wait, what?" Marcus stopped again.

"Oh I understand, not a catfish like a man pretending to be a woman, an actual catfish, out in Colorado in fact. We were on a fishing trip..."

"No! Two hundred years ago?"

George stopped on the now seemingly endless stairs and looked at him, thinking for a second and frowning, "Marcus, Di and I are over five thousand years old... We were created by the forces that be as... demigods isn't the right term, more like eternal servants, to the champion of the Gods. We have been tasked with training you and heroes like you and keeping you alive for over three hundred lifetimes."

Marcus did the math pretty quickly, "But that would mean that I have died..."

Di, who had been on the stairs behind him, rested her chin on his shoulder and spoke into his ear, "Quite a few times, you bring this up almost every lifetime that you make it to an age where you can speak and understand the gravity of death. Kallis used to be a lot more on the ball with killing you before you could walk, we had a few bad years." she pulled her head back off his shoulder and scoffed, "But hey! Last time's the charm! Am I right?"

Marcus just followed along in stunned silence as they continued down the stairs, he had wondered about the afterlife. Who hadn't. But reincarnation had been so far down the list for him that it hadn't struck him as much of an option let alone that he could be the reincarnation of a God-bound warrior who was meant to save the world. That was a bit much.

The whole mind trip that he was in kept him in a funk. He glazed through a celebratory breakfast feast, a wholesome gathering of a surprising number of people eating pancakes, waffles, bacon, and fresh eggs all stacked so high on tables that the piles of food blocked the view of people sitting across from each other. It was a huge meal but Marcus spent the better part of an hour nibbling on a waffle. People interrupted his meal with pats on the back and words of congratulations, he would nod, maybe even give the occasional smile, but he was not there. He was stuck trying to figure out what it all meant.

It wasn't until all the plates were cleared and he sat alone that he was finally able to pull it all together, he sat outside at the elongated picnic table, staring down the hill at the Bridge of Achievement. He could see, in his mind's eye, himself fighting Kallis, he saw Wallace fall. Again and again he replayed it in his head on repeat, watching it like an outside observer, until it clicked. His story was meant to be one of revenge. He smiled. For once in his life, he was happy with where it was going.

Chapter Eleven

As breakfast ended, George walked up wearing an apron and a big smile, at his side was a little girl.

"Marcus," he grinned and pushed the little girl forward, "this is Ani. She's our best Spirit Snatch player and will be teaching you about resisting Channeling. She comes to us from one of our Inuit ranches up in Northern Canada." He rustled her braided black hair a little and squished her mocha skin around her green eyes. "She is also one of our most promising healers."

Ani stepped forwards, she couldn't have been more than twelve. It took him a second to place her, but she had been the little girl from the basketball court. As George explained it, the game that Marcus had seen them play on their first day had been one that not only showed off skills, but was also one of subterfuge focused around the idea of each player trying to make an impressive basket while other players also tried to drain them of their ability to cast. The resistance of channeling was more impressive than the casting was and, as Marcus quickly learned, significantly more difficult.

Ani walked him out to the basketball court and started their game handing him the basketball to shoot. She smiled and said, "Ok, take a shot."

Marcus took the ball from her and pushed it up into the air and, with a little bit of channeling the nearby lawn, made it do a few loops in the air before landing neatly in the basket.

Ani giggled at the showmanship and matched the shot. "Good, now go again." She said, summoning the ball back to her.

So again, he moved on the court, farther away from the basket this time and turned away from his target. With a final glance over his shoulder, he threw the ball up into the air and guided it towards the basket. For added effect, he turned to Ani and looked her straight in the eyes as he did it. She squinted as she smiled back at him. Suddenly, he felt like his stomach had dropped out, his vision tunneled, he lost track of the ball, and he dropped to one knee. Ani let out a giggle.

"See!" She said, "It's harder than you think!"

They pushed through a few more baskets where he would try to make the shot and she would drain him before he could make it. Marcus moved all the way up to the bottom of the key and was unable to lift his arms up when he finally gave up.

Ani, who was proving to be as difficult a teacher as he was a student, rolled her eyes when he finally sat down to drink the juices that George had brought them during their game. "You know this is so easy that children do it as a game." Her voice was husky for a child and Marcus quickly grew to hate it.

Since it was solidified that Marcus could not play the game outright, Ani looked him over. She stepped up in front of him as he sipped his juice and took a deep breath, looking down into his eyes, she reached a hand out, as if signaling him to stop where he was, as she lifted a rock that was sitting next to him. The rock itself was smaller than a baseball but even that small amount of power that she was pulling from him was enough to make it hard for him to support himself with both arms while sitting on the ground and he fell back spilling his juice on himself.

She smiled one of her mocking grins and Marcus knew putting up with this torture would really try his self control.

"See," she said, like she had proven a point that Marcus didn't believe in. "It's easy! But it is way worse than the Drain."

Marcus scoffed, he tried to brush off the fatigue but Ani was right, being channeled felt like the stomach drop on a rollercoaster met with the hangover of a lifetime, he actually felt the power being pulled from him. For a moment he felt bad for the pigs.

"Here," She plopped down next to him and fished through her bag and pulled out an apple and offered it to him. He reached out and accepted it, taking a big bite out of it.

"No," she scolded, "channel it. You will get more energy if you do."

Marcus focused on the apple and was able to channel it without much effort and, sure enough, as he watched it wither and wrinkle, he felt better.

"Now, I want you to try to channel me," she smiled. "Don't worry, I'm good at this."

Her grin was devilish and for a moment he forgot that he was working with a child and a sense of competition overtook him. As he looked at her and readied himself, he snapped back into a moment of concern, remembering what he had done to Wallace in the Loretz.

As if she had read his mind, Ami nodded and pursed her lips, being as serious as a child could be, "It's ok, you won't be able to."

Again, Marcus was caught off guard by being mocked by a child, so he did the only thing that a maladjust who had been cast into a God war could do. He reached out and, with every bit of force that he could muster, began to focus on Ani drawing her power into him. She stumbled slightly, just enough for him to lose his concentration in fear he was hurting her and he stopped.

"Oh my God, are you ok? I'm sorry." He began moving towards her.

She wiped her eyes and laughed, "I just wanted to see how good you are. Go again, maybe try your best this time." She planted her feet and curled one extended hand at him in the universal "bring it on" gesture. She was cocky and Marcus hated cocky kids.

Once again, Marcus planted his feet and reached out, this time with both hands. He felt a little silly with the reaching to grab pose where he had no real reason to, so he put his arms back down at his sides and just focused on channeling Ani. Nothing happened. So he raised a hand, he still couldn't feel her. He brought up both hands again, his hands outstretched like he was reaching to choke her, and despite the effort that had him shaking, he still didn't feel anything. It was as if she wasn't even there.

In the effort he had closed his eyes, he stopped straining and opened one eye. It was a comic enough move that Ani, who was standing when he opened his eye, fell to the ground laughing, a childish squeal intermittently broken by snorts. When she fell, Marcus could feel her power there again and he started pulling. The moment he did he felt the source disappear again and then the flow reversed as Ani, who was still on the ground laughing, started to pull from him. Slowly at first, enough to cause a light headache, but then it felt more aggressive. He started to get tunnel vision and that's when he got a little scared.

Ani stopped laughing and stood up, bringing both of her hands, outstretched, towards him as he fell to one, and then two knees. "You weren't playing nice." By her face she was yelling, but Marcus could only hear muffled sounds as he was overcome with the sensation of being thrown into a tight ice hole in frozen water.

"I'm sorry, jeeze!" He shot back, trying to sound strong but apologetic. By the shaking in his voice it was clearly more like begging. As his consciousness flickered with long blinks he searched his mind for a way to save himself. "I don't know the rules."

She stopped channeling him and his eyesight stabilized enough that her form was able to turn back into something that was clearly human instead of the soft brown smudge it had been. She walked over to a nearby tree and pulled a basket full of fruit from a hole in the trunk and brought it over to him.

"I know," she said, frowning, "there are no rules in Spirit Snatch, only winning." That was when it dawned on Marcus what a horrible name for a children's game.

Ani leaned in and whispered, "Do you think you are ready to actually learn now?"

Marcus nodded, holding two cantaloupes as they molded and turned to mush in his hands, filling the air with a sweet and comforting smell. He was still too tired for words but was getting better.

"Ok, then," she sighed, "I want you to focus on your own energy, feel how strong you are." She took a deeper breath and brought her hands flat together in front of her, like she was praying. She took three more breaths, looping her hands in large circles to either side and bringing them back to her center prayer pose each time. "Like this." Marcus was again made very aware that he was being led by a child.

"Ok, I'll try." He pushed himself up to his feet again and followed her exact movements, albeit a little half heartedly. "Good?"

Ani scrunched up her face and walked around him taking large deliberate steps, her hands clasped behind her back like a little General. When she once again was in front of him she reached out and pulled from him, he dropped to a knee, hard. She threw him a pear and told him to try again.

The next three hours went that same way, an endless loop of Marcus trying to focus on his inner strength and then falling in one way or another, and then getting a piece of fruit to rally. By the time that George came by to announce that lunch was ready both of them were happy for a break and more than a little frustrated. Marcus was covered in cuts and bruises from falling and he was exhausted. Ani, not visibly worse for the wear, had started to lose her voice from yelling at him.

"He's hopeless!" Ani said with a big roll of her eyes and a dramatic shrug. "Are you sure this is the right guy?" She didn't wait for an answer and just walked away towards the tables where lunch was.

"Well maybe you aren't a good teacher," was all that Marcus could come up with, he looked at George with his mouth open and his arms outstretched to either side in the universal "Help me out here, man" signal, but then the moment passed and Marcus realized that he, an adult, was yelling after a child. A very strong and gifted magical child, but a child all the same.

George ignored Marcus' moment and put his hands on his hips and shrugged, looking at Ani as she walked away, "Tough one that Anirniq, isn't she?" he shook his head and looked back at Marcus. "So how about some lunch?"

Marcus' mind was in a tailspin, he snapped at George, "No! I need to learn how to stop her from channeling me, I need to learn from an adult, and I need to do that instead of having finger sandwiches and tea or whatever the heck you have planned for today!"

George put one hand softly to his heart and an exaggerated look of surprise filled his face, "Anger! Wow! What a surprise from you, Marcus. I couldn't imagine, in all of my days, that you would ruin lunch by being angry and self centered. Resisting channeling is so easy that a child can do it, Marcus. A child significantly stronger than yourself, apparently." His faked shock turned to real anger, "You know what? I'm surprised that you, having acted like a child all day today, aren't much better at this! I would actually wager that most of the children here are stronger than you! Do you know why I would bet on that, Marcus? Because, even if I didn't know them, I know you! You are new, you don't know anything and instead of living in the moment and taking in the experience you try to brute your way through everything. They are better than you! You may be meant to be a hero, but if you keep on sulking and being a petulant man baby, you will never be a hero! Dog gone it, Marcus, maybe Demi made a mistake with you!"

Marcus felt something in his stomach clench up and a dam form in his lungs, he wasn't expecting this from George and he took that hurt and wanted to pass it on.

"I never wanted this!" Marcus yelled back, once again choosing anger over apology. "I don't know why I would want to participate in a God war, I don't know if I even believe what you've told me. You, one of the people I trust most in the world, have been lying to me for the last three years. Three! Years! George!" Marcus had clenched his fists and was leaning all in into his fit. He felt like he was on the brink of going too far but he wasn't about to give up on a chance to let everything out. "I trusted you and now, you're going to be the last person I trust in this life!"

It was a death blow and Marcus knew it. Hurt filled George's eyes. Even if George had been lying the entire time Marcus knew him, he had always preached trust in Group and the passion that he had brought to healing others was far beyond anything that could be faked. This place, even, was so full of positivity and good intent, Marcus knew as soon as the words left his mouth that he would regret them, his face softened in apology but George didn't see it.

In the middle of his shouting, Marcus saw George's eyes start to tear up and he turned his back to hide his face.

"George..." Marcus started, his voice softening, immediately trying to pull back the damage that had been done.

"Marcus, if you don't want to believe that what we did came from a place of good intentions, that's fine. We meant it for the best, we didn't know what to do and thought that maybe this was the best way to get you into it this time, just ripping off the band-aid. We were wrong." He turned back to Marcus, his cheeks soaked with tears, "We have been best friends for over 100 lifetimes," he spoke with a dry mouth, "It's too bad that your last one has to be where you break that chain." His sobbing turned to a blubbering yell, "And if you want to just curl up in your bed and wait for death to take you away, go for it! This world isn't worth saving anymore."

"George I..." Marcus stammered, he couldn't think of a time that he had hurt someone like this. He didn't know what to say.

George's face straightened and his breath calmed. "You know what, Marcus? Right now I don't care. Whatever you want to say, we can just talk later once we have both calmed down."

Again, Marcus found himself speechless.

"Do you know why I loved coming to Group?" He asked.

Marcus shook his head, shame locking his lips.

"Because even though you didn't know who you were meant to be, or who I really was, I got to see my best friend get better every day. I got to see you be happy and help others where you knew they would never help you. I got to know the Ra'Saram that I have loved for hundreds of years. The amazing partner that Di and I have dedicated our lives to. Seeing you finally have a life and love. Seeing you see your value. It was an amazing journey for me." His voice cracked and he looked over at the people who were gathering at the lunch tables. "I have to go and splash some water on my face, I have an entire group to take care of and the..." he paused, "finger sandwiches and *lemonade* won't serve themselves."

He turned his back and walked off, Marcus wanted to call after him but didn't know what he could say that could possibly make the betrayal any better so instead he headed back to his room, thinking that maybe curling up and dying might just be the right move. He walked up the stairs and laid down in his bed, throwing the soft comforter over his head like a funeral shroud, and let his mind wander.

Chapter Twelve

The bed was charmed to warm quickly to a comfortable temperature and Marcus made sure to lock the door before allowing himself to fully give into his wallowing self pity. A thought spiral of negativity engulfed him as he replayed the argument with George in his head, the image of George's swollen face caught in his mind, looking more and more sad as he saw him in his mind's eye, the pain that he realized he had caused to George seemed to push back into him ten fold. A few times a couple tears ran down his face as he tried to push past the guilt, but there was no respite in his mind, no matter how much he tossed and turned.

As he took on his inner demons, he listened to the lunch happening outside, a non-stop roar of laughter and happy conversation. He could picture the children running around the table and the piles of sandwiches that George had made. His stomach let out a loud growl as he realized that he still hadn't eaten yet. For a moment he considered getting up and going out to grab something, but the thought of facing George right now seemed a bit too daunting.

"Just go and apologize." He said to himself, trying to rally around the idea of being the bigger man. It wasn't even a scenario that called for being the bigger man, he knew that he had screwed up and that it was all his fault, George owed him nothing. He sat back down.

He watched as shadows covered the window. "Perfect," he groaned at the world that seemed to be reflecting his current mood. It better not be a charm, like some environmental mood ring, but he was not going to put it past Demi that the ranch had some sort of empath powers that would mirror something in him just to make things more difficult to hide.

Marcus could hear her voice in his head, "Smile or you'll bring darkness into the world." or something on brand like that.

Then there was a loud bang and the laughter outside turned to screams, another series of loud explosions shook the farm house and Marcus threw himself from the bed to the window and looked out.

A mass of angry storm clouds had overtaken the sunny day, casting the ranch into a dark shadow. Marcus leapt back as a table, food and all, flew through the air and shattered into thousands of pieces against the house just under his window. The people who were at the table were scattering as two purple bolts of energy hurtled towards them and hit the house which rippled with blue energy.

Marcus saw George standing at the front of the group, between the group and the source of the bolts, but, from the window, he could not make out who was firing them.

"Everyone get inside, get behind the barrier!" George shouted, waving his arms around in a frenzy of spells as another barrage of bolts flew towards him, a few making impact and sending light cascading around his body. He didn't move an inch, holding his ground against the onslaught and shielding the people who were running to gather the children and run them inside. A few bodies were already scattered, motionless on the ground.

Then the attackers came into view, and without a second thought, Marcus turned from the window and started sprinting down the stairs to get outside. No fewer than a dozen crimson robed figures stepped into view accompanied by none other than Kallis who floated a few feet in the air behind the line of them, a vibrant smile on his face, black flowing robes giving him the appearance of being surrounded by water.

From the stairwell, Marcus could hear Kallis, "Hello Georgie, haven't I killed you yet?"

Marcus made it out the door as George shot back, "I can't seem to remember a time that you have, Kallis. Seems that you were never good enough."

Kallis let out a chuckle, "Well maybe this time we

shake things up. Whadda ya say?"

"I thought you'd never ask." George smirked.

It was then that both of them noticed that Marcus had come outside. Kallis was the first to speak.

"Then again, we could save a lot of bloodshed if you just handed him over. I know you don't believe it, but I'd really rather not kill everyone here today. I mean, some day they will likely worship me." He grinned and offered his hand, like George was going to literally hand Marcus to him.

"You know I'd sacrifice everyone here to save Marcus!" George yelled. It struck Marcus how true that seemed and he felt another pang of guilt as he met George's eyes, the hurt still raw in them.

"That's all I've ever wanted you to do," Kallis said and he reeled back hissing to the sky which began to swirl into a black spiral overhead. It looked like the beginnings of a massive tornado from a science fiction movie.

"Get inside!" George yelled to Marcus. "Find Di, tell her to find the Sisters. I'll hold off Kallis for as long as I can." His face was fierce, his teeth clenched, but his eyes were sad.

"George, I'm not leaving you!" Marcus yelled.

"Yes you are!" George yelled at him and turned to him, throwing his arms towards him and pushing an invisible force at Marcus that blasted him off his feet and back into the house, the door slamming shut. Marcus got up as he heard the ripping sound of spells flying through the air and yells from multiple voices that Marcus didn't recognize. He tried the door but it would not reopen.

"What are you doing?" Di said from behind him. "We've got to go!"

"George is still out there!" Marcus yelled, not turning around, "He said he was going to hold him off! We have to help him!"

Di hesitated and Marcus heard her breath catch in her throat. "Then we have to go." she said solemnly.

Marcus fought with the door, pulling against it, able to get a small line of light to push its way through. "Help me get this open!" he yelled, not looking back.

"We have to go!" She repeated, more forcefully this time. Marcus looked back and Di was glaring at him, tears in her eyes. "Now!"

"I'm not going to leave him!" He yelled, focusing on the energy that the protective locks had formed and drawing it in. His skin started to glow with the same blue of the house as he pulled. He was amazed at the sensation of strength that it gave him as it coursed through him. He had never felt this powerful before, not by a long shot and the energy the feeling brought him back to the Loretz, to the last time that he killed Kallis, it gave him an idea.

"Di! If I can channel the rest of the house I think I can kill him!" He yelled over the buzzing of the siphoned energy crackling out around him, long transparent sparks of energy leaping from him and leaving scorch marks scattered on the carpeted floor.

"If you channel the entire house it will leave us vulnerable, we will all die! You have to stop! There is no way that you could handle that much power!" Di was now pleading but Marcus didn't care, he kept going. "You'll die!"

Di reached out to grab him but a band of energy leapt from him and knocked her back. He didn't have control of the power, it felt like he had lost control of a spell that he didn't even cast. He turned back to apologize, but after seeing the look of betrayal on her face, it was remarkably similar to the one that he had seen on George no more than an hour ago.

"Fine!" she shouted from the floor. "This is as good a way as any to let the world fall to trash. If you want to die alone, this is the place to do it! The hill has a great view for the ashes that will be scattered into the wind when Kallis is done with you. If you want to live, meet us in the basement. Just do me a favor and stop sucking all of the power out of our last chance at saving ourselves." She pointed to the blue translucent force field that was now flickering in front of him. "It isn't an infinite source, just a roadblock. All you have to do is ask it to let you out, it will let you."

Marcus stared for a second at the door, able only to see bolts flying through the air, at least that was a good sign, if there was still a battle going on, George was still alive. He nodded back at Di, but she had already turned and left, heading down the stairs to whatever the basement held.

"I would like to leave," Marcus said to the door, "please." He added unsure if that would make a difference.

Sure enough, the door flew open and the energy that was there shimmered for a second but did not disappear. Marcus took a step through and felt as though he had been plunged into an ice bucket. The chill was painful and immediately cut to the bone, but he was able to step out into the afternoon light just in time to see George, who was pinned down behind a picnic table that was being magically anchored to the ground by a series of red strands that had taken the form of chain links that stretched into the ground.

George looked up and saw him and shook his head, "For the love of... Marcus get inside!"

Marcus looked around, frozen in place for a moment of happiness as he saw George still alive. The moment was pulled away from him as a bolt of green light flickered past his head, led by a screaming skull made of light which bit at the side of his face as it flew past, narrowly missing, its jaw clacking in his ear as it snapped at him. He made the twenty foot sprint to the overturned table and dove as another barrage of crackling whisps flew past him.

"What the hell are you doing?" George yelled at him, more than loud enough for Marcus to hear him. "This isn't the hill you want to die on." a smile cracked across his face as he laughed at his own pun, an expression that Marcus hadn't thought that he would ever see again.

"I wasn't going to let you die alone," Marcus said. "If I am meant to be the saviour of the world, the Gods won't let me die now." He tried a little gallows humor but it didn't land.

George shook his head, "It doesn't work... you know what, forget it! If you are going to be out here, you might as well be useful. Watch this!" He started moving his fingers in a way that seemed inhuman to Marcus and a series of red strands connected between his hands forming a cask of some kind. With a grunt, George hefted the barrel over the table and stood up clenching a fist forcefully towards it causing it to explode near the group of now only six hooded figures, two of them getting thrown through the air and down the hill out of sight. Marcus realized that Kallis was not among them.

"Where is Kallis, did you kill him?"

George shook his head again, taking cover and pulling Marcus down with him, "I don't know where he went, once the fighting started he disappeared. I need you to start fighting if you are going to be out here, there are only four left."

Marcus grinned, it seemed as though George had already forgiven him, but he apologized for good measure, "George, I'm..."

"That better end with 'working on a spell to kill the last of them' or I'm not interested." he snapped, proving Marcus wrong in his timing.

So he snapped to and started trying to move his fingers like George had shown him to no avail. A few wisps of red light jumped between his fingers as he tried to get it right but there was nothing connecting. He then threw his hands up in frustration and stood up, focusing on one of the cultists and reached out and started to channel him, his already overflowing energy crackling out around him, with another hand he reached towards the second closest robed assailant and both of them dropped to a knee as he pulled the life out of them.

The other two started throwing magic at him but each bolt that came towards him was absorbed by the blue light that was streaming from his body. Marcus smiled as the two he was channeling continued dropping to the ground and he felt the energy leave them. He then focused on the energy that was flying off him and he shot it all forward at the last two, beams of pure white light coming from his hands in an unstopping beam and he watched as it shot through the two cultists, cutting a hole through them and, as they dropped, continued slicing up through them leaving nothing but two legs that fell to the ground motionless.

Marcus turned to George with a big smile and reached out to hug George, he was a little proud of his casting, however exhausted the beam had left him. The excitement didn't last for long as he stood in horror as Kallis materialized behind George. What happened next happened all in slow motion for Marcus. He watched as Kallis slowly went from being semi-transparent to fully materializing. Marcus reached out towards George who, incorrectly, thought he was going for a hug and stretched his arms out wide. Marcus tried to summon some energy from his reserves but didn't find enough energy to expend on anything besides a few small sparks that Kallis absorbed without issue. George's smile stretched from cheek to cheek in a falsely assumed victory, his face turned to one of contorted fear and confusion as Marcus saw his chest start to glow. In his last moments George didn't understand what was happening and his face gave away a sense of betrayal thinking it was Marcus that was killing him. Then he turned to the source of pain as his shirt tore.

The moments before George's death were a flurry of mixed emotions but he died with a look of suffering and pain.

Marcus yelled at the top of his lungs at George, something to the effect of "NO!" but it came out as a gag. One of the worst parts of magical wounds was that they immediately cauterized making the wounds seem less fatal, regardless of whether or not they were killing blows. This one was. George reached out and with both hands, his arms stuck between reaching out for a hug of victory and a plea for aid. His eyes met Marcus' and he blinked for the last time as his chest ruptured and light poured out in a continuous and straight line and Marcus caught him. George's face contorted in a frozen and permanent plea for help that broke Marcus' heart.

Kallis stood behind George, a massive grin on his face, "Goodbye, George." his face was full of satisfaction as Marcus felt the full dead weight of George press against him, knocking him back to the ground and pinning him down.

Marcus pushed against George, trying to get up but couldn't budge him. His energy sapped, all he could do was watch as Kallis loomed over him poised, like a snake ready to strike.

"Well Marcus, it looks like it is time to say goodbye, again, for the last time." Kallis smirked. With a sigh he added "It feels good to finally be over this." and he started to gather a ball of black energy in a small orb that floated around his fingers, wisps of white flitting off it. He raised his hand, the spell with it, and moved it towards Marcus slowly and paused, "It almost feels sad to think that this really is the end." and he looked at the ball, a real sadness in his eyes. "I wanted so much to have our big end. Too bad." He shrugged and continued to bring the orb closer to Marcus, who was still struggling to get out from under George.

Then, before Kallis could make his move, Marcus felt himself being pulled along the grass at a high speed towards the house. Kallis threw the ball at him but it didn't land as Marcus slid through the open door that slammed shut behind him. Marcus looked around to find what had pulled him and saw Di, her face streaked with tears, just finishing up whatever spell had pulled him in.

"Di, you came back." Marcus said meekly.

"We have to go," Di said in a calm, even tone.

"I'm sorry." He wasn't going to miss another opportunity to say it.

"It doesn't matter, we just need to go. He knew what he was getting into out there." She let out a brief sob, catching the next one in her throat, "Kallis will be able to break the shield, let's get out of here." she turned and started making her way to the basement.

"If he is coming in, we can fight him here." Marcus insisted. "We know he is coming through the door." As if on cue there was a loud slam at the door as the wall rippled with blue protective energy.

"We can't fight him, we can't win, not now. You are too weak and I am too distracted." She said and started down the stairs.

"If we go downstairs we will just have to fight him when he gets in anyway!"

"The basement has a teleportation sigil, it's how we got you here before. It's our only hope for escape. We will have to destroy it on the way out. The Ranch is lost." she shook her head admitting defeat.

Marcus followed Di down the stairs and into the basement where a series of large stone pillars stood, each of them with ornate carvings and painted symbols. In the middle of the ring of pillars was a circle drawn on the floor.

Di offered Marcus her hand, "Come on, if we take it together I don't have to worry about where you end up."

Marcus took her hand and they stepped into the ring. Marcus heard a loud popping sound as they stepped into the center of the circle and with a snap of her fingers, Di activated the sigils and the stones lit up as light ran along the floor to their feet. With another wave of her hand, Di sent a crack running through the ceiling of the basement and it started caving in, the whole house collapsing above them just as they were sucked out of the room.

Chapter Thirteen

Instantaneously, Marcus and Di appeared in an old subway terminal surrounded by the refugees of the Ranch. A few of them scurried back and forth to various people who were leaning against the red brick walls and tended to the various wounds. Marcus spotted Ani and Lance were standing at a makeshift platform working on taking care of Charles, who had a bleeding gash on his forehead.

Mick waddled up to Di from Charles' side, concern on his face and a bottle of some clear brown liquid in his hand. "George?" he asked.

Di just shook her head and Mick pursed his lips and gave her a knowing nod. Then poured a little of his drink on the ground and walked away. Marcus watched as the liquor pooled in the tile floor.

"It isn't safe here." Di announced to the group, doing her best to keep her head up and look at them. There were only a few who were able to lift their heads up enough to see her anyway. "George spent a long time preparing us for this, we knew this day would come and are as ready as we could possibly be. We know the plan. Everyone starts following their paths, we will meet in the *pages of our next chapter.*" She accentuated the last words and a few people nodded as they turned and drew a sigil on the wall, glowing light emitting from each and groups started making their way into the light and silently disappearing. Within a few moments, the hundred or so people had disappeared leaving behind a small group that was looking expectantly at Di.

Di nodded at them and turned and silently traced her finger on the wall in the shape of her own.

"Come on, everyone. Time to go." she said as she stepped through.

The next few days were spent trying to avoid any pursuit mounted by Kallis. The group, having patched themselves up, made their way through a series of teleportation sigils that created a maze through various parts of the state, sometimes ending on a farm, an abandoned warehouse, and once a retired water treatment plant. Each time they bounced, Di made sure to destroy where they had come through.

"Each location has several sigils to a network of other places. A few more jumps and we should be untraceable." Di explained to Marcus. Those were the only words that she, or anyone said to Marcus in those fear drenched days. They stayed on the move, sometimes traveling by foot a few miles to find their next stop. With children in tow, moving from place to place took much longer than it should have and everyone was constantly on high alert.

They finally stopped in an old bookstore called The Split Binding, a poorly lit shop with dust covered stacks. As they arrived, Marcus saw that they were the last to get there and saw that a new face had joined the masses. Running from group to group, talking to the drawn and concerned faces was the shop owner, a portly woman with curly brown hair that welcomed them with a grim smile and moved towards Di first, greeting her with a big motherly hug. It seemed that news travels fast in magical circles.

"Di!" She said, both of them hiding their faces in the hug. "I'm so sorry to hear about George. You know I always loved you two."

"He always thought so highly of you, too, Clara. He never would have trusted you with all of our lives had he not held you dear to his heart." she pulled back her head and turned to the crowd. "Everyone, this place is safe, but we do have to stay indoors for now. Clara has been kind enough to offer us shelter, please find a place to settle in, we are going to be here for a while."

After that, the two disappeared and everyone did as they were told, gathering into small groups and finding places to set up bedrolls and makeshift cots.

Marcus saw Clara and Di whispering behind the

checkout counter at the front of the store. As he approached the old wooden desk, they stopped and looked away from him. "Di, George told me to find the Sisters? I think that…" but before he could finish they peeled away from each other and walked away from him, not stopping until they were no longer in his sight. Ever since George had died that was all he had gotten, frowns, silence, and no one making eye contact.

The refugees gathered in the corners of the store and leaned up in the stacks, making small camp circles, keeping their voices low as if Kallis might be just a few stacks over looking for them. After a few more failed attempts to get Di or Clara's attention, in frustration, Marcus pulled a book from the shelves and dropped it. The slam was met by a few gasps as it broke the silence of the shop. The only attention he would directly receive the few times that he tried the disruption, was from Clara, who would always show up a few seconds later to shush him and then walk away. It became a little bit of a game for Marcus to see how loud of a sound would summon her and how quickly she could find him. Without fail a few seconds after he made a sound loud enough to get her attention, Clara would poke her head around and, finger pressed to her lips, shoot him a scolding shush.

After a week of silence, Marcus started to fall in with the rest of the group, silently sitting, pressed against the rows of books. He started pulling them and reading through whatever covers he enjoyed. He had never been a big reader, he loved the idea but life always seemed to get in the way. The escapism of reading had really piqued his interest as he had been barred from any attempts at leaving and had no one else to engage with.

The first book that he pulled was a fantasy novel about a boy and his dragon and their fight to save the realm against an evil force looking to conquer it. He blew through it in a matter of hours and laughed and cried as he envisioned Di as his dragon on his own quest. It was a stretch but it struck him just right. The rest of the series took less than a day to read through since he had no distractions.

Another week went by and Marcus had moved into the more gritty fantasies, some now banned books that involved magic users who hunted demons of Victorian England for a living and a few about people throughout the ages who had used magic to mount other battles against evil. All along the way picturing himself as the hero in each story, living, through his mind's eye, each situation clinging to the side of his proverbial seat.

It was when he finished the final book in a series about a medieval caster who had discovered that she was a magical protector of a great weapon meant to free the country from a great evil that he had had enough. Each book increased his desire to take the next step, each protagonist pushing past their failures. He couldn't take sitting anymore so he pushed himself up from the nook that he had claimed as "Camp Marcus" and made his way to the front where Clara perched all day.

"I'm done waiting around for Kallis to find us!" He said, his voice coming out of him much louder than he intended, it had been a few days since he had last spoken. He coughed and adjusted his volume to a quieter but equally stern tone, "I cannot let George have died in vain. We have to take this fight to Kallis. Where is Di?"

"She's getting a car." Clara said, not looking up from the book that she was reading on the counter in front of her.

Marcus was surprised, he hadn't heard her leave and didn't entirely expect an actual response having received nothing more than a "Shh!" in ages.

"She left a few hours ago to get a car for your trip to meet the Sisters. I have deemed you ready." She said, equally as plainly as before, if not a little bit more curtly.

Marcus felt every eye in the bookstore on him. Looking over his shoulder he saw eyes poking out from above books on shelves and heads peeking around corners to listen in. "I'm... wait what?" he stammered.

"What part of that confuses you, hun? The car you need to see the Sisters that George insisted you see? Or that I have deemed you worthy of meeting them?" She looked up from her book, meeting Marcus' eye and giving him a glare that made him very aware that she hadn't wanted to stop reading.

When he didn't respond she continued, "Because you have read the texts by your own choice. You know what you must know to be a hero. Sacrifice, pain, suffering.You could have chosen any books here and you were drawn to stories about yourself. Your past lives. Sure they are some rewrites of history where you actually succeeded but you were drawn to them, and because of that I have given Di the direction to the first task on your path to the Gates." She nodded, affirming that she was happy with the explanation that she had given and went back to her book.

Behind him, Marcus heard a collective sigh and, for the first time in two weeks, the survivors of the Ranch started talking amongst themselves at a regular volume.

"But... what?" Marcus pressed.

"Di can fill you in, clearly the stories are true, you have always lacked patience." Clara scoffed.

Di walked in the front door, causing the little bells in the frame to jingle.

She shook some keys in her hand and smiled, "Road trip!"

Chapter Fourteen

Marcus and Di loaded into an old Mercury Sable that smelled heavily of fresh dirt and rust and spent a few minutes in silence as they started driving down the road. They drove past a "Now Leaving Ithaca" sign heading North.

"Where are we going?" Marcus finally broke the silence.

"Syracuse." Di said, "Clara has given us the location of the Sisters." She looked at Marcus, completely missing her normal look of mischievous glee. "No reason you should know who they are, but they are pretty much the reason that you would envision a coven to be made up of three witches. They are as immortal as they come and were one of the worst creations that the Gods have ever made. But they have been around long enough to be able to know a ton, Clara is essentially their secretary. She serves as a scribe to the Gods as well as a gatekeeper to the Sisters. She's pretty much the only way to gain access to them without being guaranteed a slow and painful death. They should know where the first Gate is for you to complete. A way for you to start getting a leg up on Kallis."

"Oh," Marcus was surprised at how well that answered all of the questions in his head, "Have you met them before?"

"I have done everything in my power to not meet with them more than I have had to." She said. "They are horrible tricksters and cruel witches. They use each other's power to channel and have become twisted versions of the power trinity that they had first been designed to be. They were created to be guardians of the wild but instead, thanks to some genius' idea of granting free will, they are now the reason for the majority of woodland hauntings in the Americas and Japan. Are you familiar with Croatoan?" she asked, more caught up in the story than actually interested in him giving an answer.

"Not in the slightest."

"Well in the 1590's there was a group of settlers who came over to the new world, they settled a colony called Roanoke. Popular knowledge says that when the followup group arrived to join them, they found the fort abandoned with the word 'Croatoan' carved into the door and 'Cro' carved into a tree. Over one hundred people had vanished." She looked at him for any response but Marcus didn't have any to give so she continued.

"Most people believe that it was either disease or violence that took them out. They had done the classic colonist thing and really pissed off the local tribe, the Croatoan. But that's what happens when you show up and take what isn't yours. As it ends up that this small tribe had been pretty devout to their God. They were led by a group of individuals called Wereowances, in Algonquain it means "he who is rich" and most historians thought that to be a monetary value, but of course they are wrong." She rolled her eyes. "These individuals were rich in devotion to their God, as well as their respect for nature and were able to call upon the powers of nature and God to aid their cause, most often the protection of the tribe."

"Well, the Croatoan were a hearty agricultural people, they were of the land and by it and believed in the immortality of the soul. Their devout respect for the land gained them favor with the local forest wardens, the Sisters, and when the people of Roanoke began to push their luck... well the old Crows stepped in to solve the problem in the name of the Wereowances. By all accounts it was a massacre. The Sisters guided the forces of nature to their will, the siege only lasted a few minutes and they didn't stand a chance. The Colonists were claimed by the ground they stood upon, the sun blacked out by swarms of crows, rats came in waves, and well..." she looked over at Marcus as if she were stating the obvious, "there were the bears. Those Sisters love bear attacks. Just plain unfair if you ask me, but it is what it is, nature always wins."

"Oh, ok." Marcus said, staring out the window, watching as the city turned to forest as they headed north towards the Finger Lakes. The explosion of yellows, oranges, and reds in the trees was beautiful and, as he played with the reality of who he was about to meet, he figured it would likely be the last Fall that he would ever get to see.

After a few minutes of driving, Di broke the silence. "Oh perfect!" she said excitedly and swerved the car to the side of the road, a man hitch-hiking waved and came running up to Marcus' window.

"Where ya heading?" Di asked with an unusually kind tone.

"North to the future!" The man chuckled in a southern drawl, "How about y'all?"

He was a good looking, muscular man with a natural charm that Marcus felt was a bit off putting, he had a scruffy brown beard but was relatively clean for a hitchhiker.

"Sounds like you're going our way, we can take you as far as Syaracuse." She smiled and Marcus looked at her, unhappy with taking on a stranger and confused by her sudden willingness to pick up a complete stranger to come along on their quest.

The man took off his backpack and threw it, along with a guitar, into the back seat and climbed in. "My name is Clint." he said in a thick Texas drawl, "Been thumbing my way up here since Texas!"

"Well it's nice to meet you, Clint!" Di said, again suspiciously cheerfully, "And what are you doing in these parts?" her voice started to take on its own drawl.

"What are you doing?" Marcus hissed at her.

She slapped his chest, "Don't be rude, Marcus. We are all just people looking to get by out there. We should always help humanity when we can."

"Well, thanks sweetheart'! Been lookin' for work, makin' my way upstate. I heard there are some good ranch gigs. My old lady pushed me out, said I drank too much," he unironically pulled a beer can from his bag and popped it open, "You don't mind do ya, little lady?"

Di smiled past the term, "No worries, drink up!"

Marcus hated everything about this, but did his best to stay pleasant with their addition. Maybe Di just needed another body in the car to make her feel like George was there. Marcus wasn't sure how he felt about the fact that George would now have to be an alcoholic deadbeat hitch-hiker. But in honoring his memory, he wanted to let her heal in her own way. To each their own.

After his third beer, Clint picked up the guitar and started playing. He insisted that it would be his payment for the ride since he didn't have any money, but Marcus really wished that they could just call it a free ride once the gravely notes of his voice filled the car. It was 30 minutes of non-stop misheard lyrics greats like John Denver's Take Me Home Country Road.

Towards the end of the third singing of the worst rendition of "Friends in Low Places" that Marcus had ever heard they turned onto Cedarcrest Road and Clint stopped suddenly.

"What did you say?" he asked, his head snapping from side to side, looking for someone who wasn't there.

Neither Marcus nor Di had said anything. "We didn't say anything." Marcus said, now sure that they were in danger from the drunk hearing things in the back.

He cautiously turned around to give Clint a calming gaze and also make sure that he didn't have a weapon and watched as Clint dropped his guitar and grabbed his head.

"Pull over!" He yelled, "My head is killing me, I think I'm going to..."

He didn't get the chance to finish the sentence when his neck made a loud cracking sound and bent at an unnatural angle.

He opened his mouth and an echoing female voice came out, "Hello, Di." it said.

"Hey ya old crow. How're ya doin'?"

Chapter Fifteen

Marcus sat in the car, mouth agape as he stared back at Clint's animated corpse as it waggled its tongue around as if it were getting a feel of it for the first time. After a few seconds of flapping around, Clint let out a trilling sound and smiled.

"Ahhh." he gasped, "Been a long time, Di. I see this time you brought a gift." The female voice was raspy as if it had once been smooth but now had the texture of silk running over rough gravel. "It…" she ran her hands over the body in admiration and let out a belch, "It feels broken." Clint's face frowned.

"We're working on some short notice, Jostine." Di said

back without looking away from the road. There was a loud bang as a crow flew into the window. She coughed visibly choking back her need for added sarcasm, "Clara said that you could help."

"You only ever come to us when you want something." She frowned and leaned forwards, putting her hands around Marcus' chest. "Oh I like this one! He has a power to him! Let me trade up and I'll tell you whatever you want." Marcus felt a very wet tongue running up his neck and the sandpaper beard brushed against his cheek. Despite every urge he didn't recoil, not knowing the protocol of this kind of situation.

Di shook her head, "Sorry Jo, not this one, he is the Ra'Saram." Clint's eyes went wide. "He's the reason I'm here."

Jostine cooed and drummed Clint's fingers, "The Ra'Saram you say?" She frowned and fell back in her seat and crossed her arms, "Fine, just pull over and I'll call my sisters, anything for old Demi." She smiled a coy grin that didn't fit properly on Clint's face contorting it into a very uncomfortable wrinkle, a little bit of dip fell out of their lip.

"You and I both know that we can't do that. I stop this car and I'll be stuck with another corpse to get rid of. You can fool me once, but not this time. I have twelve more curves left with you." Jostine harrumphed and another crow hit the car window making Marcus jump.

"Fine!" she said, rolling her eyes. "What do you want to know? It's been ages since I've gotten to do anything fun, it's just been haunting after haunting. You know people just don't like camping like they used to and come out with their phones and gadgets just trying to catch a glimpse of us. Not a single one of them actual believers, none of 'em scared for a second. I could kill fifty people on this road only to have one hundred more trying to find me tomorrow. You'd think that..."

"I know what you are trying to do, Jo." Di frowned in the mirror. "I also know I just have to keep the car rolling to keep you in, don't make me take us to a crawl, neither of us want to be here."

"You never call, you never write, you know I've known you your entire life and I haven't even got a Christmas card."

"You know I must have misplaced the address, Jo. Maybe I can get that from you later." Di slowed the car down considerably and two more crows slammed into the door. "So whaddya say? Got time for a few questions?"

"Sure, sure! How about a tit for tat? One for one as it goes? You first, I know the drill."

"Fine," Di shot back a bit over confidently, Marcus was shocked at her complete lack of regard for this being that had just killed a man in their back seat and took over his body. She seemed more annoyed than grateful. "Where do we need to go for the First Gate?"

Jo smacked her lips, and thought. "Hmmmm. Starting with the big one's eh?" She let out a long, beer scented, sigh. The pupils in her eyes whited over and she opened her mouth and spoke, lips unmoving like a fleshy old school record player and her voice boomed.

"Clip clop and tick tock,

don't watch the cock or you will drop.

Find me in an apple and bring me a mirror,

show me myself because that's what I fear.

My father's a rooster and my mother's a snake,

pop goes the weasel is the poem it takes.

Reach what you seek, the jewel in my crown,

Merily merily, we all fall down."

When she finished the car fell into silence. Di shook her head, "Really? Belvedere? Thanks, Jo, I hate it."

Marcus finally found his voice, "Belvedere Castle? What does that have to..."

"Quiet boy!" Jo bellowed, her voice shaking the car and a few more crows slamming into the window causing fractures to spider out to the edges "It's my turn for questions, you can ask next if you want to use one of sweet Di's questions." Marcus shut up. "So where is that sweet husband of yours? Finally found his way out?"

Di shuddered and slammed on the breaks, "Well that's enough for today, thanks for stopping by!"

When the car came to a full stop, Jostine let out a scream as a murder of crows flew against the front window, slamming again and again against the glass as it cracked and then shattered, more crows pouring in until they filled the car. Marcus struggled with his seatbelt as he tried to make a break from the car but Di grabbed him.

"If you leave this car you die." she shook her head through the impenetrable cloud of crows. Marcus could barely make out her face but the look he did see made him believe her instantly. So he sat, birds beating against him, the gargling scream coming from the back seat grew in volume until, finally, silence.

Marcus spun around to see what happened but there was nothing but feathers and blood in the back seat. Clint's body, much like the windshield, was gone.

"Ok, what the hell was that?" He said to Di.

"Oh... yeah... that was my mom." Di shrugged and made a u-turn.

Marcus sat back in his seat, covered in glass and blood, after a quick spot check he realized that none of it was his own. "Well, she seemed... interesting."

"She's an old Hag from the beginning. I didn't tell you who she was to me because it wasn't relevant." she sighed, "That and I knew that she was going to do something massively theatrical and that it would scare the crap out of you." She laughed, "You had that one coming."

Marcus felt sick to his stomach, the smell of the crow

blood made him realize what had just happened. "... and Clint? You brought her, what? A sacrifice?"

"More or less, we told you I'm an empath, right?" She picked up speed again, heading back down the road. "I could feel his intentions a mile before we picked him up. Never pick up hitch-hikers, that guy was a full on killer." She shook her head. "We had about another two miles down this road before he was going to off both of us. That was his thing. My mother would have loved that, finding my body in a car on the side of *her* road. She would find a way to the afterlife just to remind me that a murdering hitchhiker that I let into my car killed me."

"Huh. Does she... uh... live around here?" Marcus gestured around to the general forest at large.

"The Gods found that they could set boundaries for her and my aunts. They do it to keep them apart so that they can't wreak anymore havoc. Mommy dearest is contained to the northeast for the most part, although I have heard that she has found a way to make it all around the United States. As long as they are kept apart, they are another horror that the world won't have to deal with. Alone, they mostly like to try and scare folks. Taking a body is their only way of staying anywhere for extended periods. This stretch of road is one of her regular haunts, she dresses up like a lady in a wedding dress and tries to cause car crashes. She manages that quite a bit but when she takes a body she gets trapped where they are until the car stops or the road ends. Then the..."

"Crows... yeah." Marcus Interrupted. He swallowed hard and looked around, feeling like there was something watching him from the woods.

"Don't worry," Di said, seeing him looking around. "They are only able to take on bodies where the soul has been brutally compromised. It leaves a void that can be filled and they jump in and push out what there was."

Marcus nodded and accepted this as the truth and braced himself as the cold that was now pouring through the windshield wrapped itself around him. As they drove he channeled trees and plants to keep himself warm.

Once they were back off Cedarcrest, Di pulled off to the side of the road and chuckled at Marcus as he shivered. "You still have the instincts of a newborn, seriously!" She waved her hand and, like the plate that he had broken, the thousands of pieces of glass lifted from the car and placed themselves back into the windshield.

Marcus winced as a few of them pulled out of the skin on his face and arms in spots that he hadn't realized had been punctured.

"Sorry," Di apologized half heartedly, a few shards pulling from her body as well.

"It's whatever," Marcus shook it off. "So where to next?"

"We've got about two hundred and fifty miles of trip ahead of us," she said, looking out at the road as she started back to driving. "We're going home."

Chapter Sixteen

They made the ride back into the city in relative silence. Di turned on the radio to the local rock station and sang along with most songs. Marcus finally broke the silence after about an hour of trying to find the right thing to ask.

"So that poem she said. What was that?"

"My mother… ugh I hate that… Jo loves to speak in prophecies. She can actually give the straight answer but was always one with a flair for the dramatic." She gestured to the back seat as if that proved her point. "More or less, she was saying that the Cockatrice at Belvedere Castle has something to do with the first gate." She shrugged, "Makes sense, Jacob Mould was obsessed with the occult, I just figured that it would be something older."

"And we are supposed to? What? Go into the castle and find the gate? I've walked through there hundreds of times, nothing ever happened. Millions of people a year go there."

"Well, she didn't say how to open the gate, only that it was there and that we have to show it's reflection. Sounds like we are going to fight it."

"And how are we supposed to do that?" Marcus asked, wracking his memory for anything related to the Cockatrice from his Dungeons and Dragons days when he was a kid. There was nothing there.

"Well the cockatrice is a dragon with a rooster head, touching it, looking at it in the eye, or letting it breathe on you will kill you instantly. So we probably won't win up close but if we can't look at it we probably can't get it from too far away either. We need a rooster."

"A what?"

"A rooster, it's crow will kill the thing in a heartbeat. That's easy!"

"And where will we get a rooster?"

Di looked around on the road for a second, "Good point, probably not a lot of options. We could swing off and raid a farm real quick?" Then she shook her head. "Probably not worth the stop. We can just show it it's reflection and that will kill it too. Something about the penetrating gaze of death." she chuckled. "This is when we could have used George, he always was able to plan for things like this." Her face fell.

Marcus realized that he had never asked her how she was doing, "How, um, have you been, ah, been holding up?"

"I'm fine," she clearly lied. "We both knew that this was an inevitability. You just start to think that after a few thousand years that maybe the Goddess actually gave you something special. We made it out of so many scrapes together I thought... maybe..." her voice trailed off.

"Maybe what?" Marcus wanted to comfort her and watching her start to cry broke his heart a little.

"You'll laugh, but we had made it out of so many things that we never should have been able to, so many dungeons, so many fights that we watched you die in. I thought that we might have been Gods all along and that we just hadn't been told. Like it was some sort of a test to prove that we were worthy." She laughed the kind of laugh that comes out when your nose is clogged, a broken laugh that conveyed no humor. It was a laugh of self loathing.

Marcus couldn't find the words to comfort her, and instead, humorously, said, "Well could you imagine? I could only picture the people who would worship you. I mean George, he had the charisma, but you would end up with a bunch of punk rock mall rats worshipping you. They would make offerings to you the same way they give cigarettes to the one hot girl in their group." He laughed and she chuckled along. "No robes for your group, everyone would just be wearing black skinny jeans and band shirts."

She glared at him through running makeup, "And what's wrong with band shirts and skinny jeans?" She was joking with him but there was a slight twinge of defensiveness.

"Nothing," he laughed. "I could see it now, 'Worship Di! Goddess of Hot Topic, Ruler of the Food Court'!" He crossed his right arm across his chest, clenching a fist to his heart, and the left arm he held up in a fist, extending his pinky and index finger into the Sign of the Horns.

She snorted a genuine laugh, "Shut up!" She grabbed a handful of wrappers from the cup holder and threw them at him and then turned up the music and rolled down both windows letting the sound billow out and the cold air pour in. Marcus watched her for a few minutes, it was good to see her smile again. Even if they were a few hours from certain death.

"What are you looking at?" Di finally said to him, realizing that he was watching her.

"Thank you, Di." he said, staring her in the eyes.

"You know what, Golden Boy?" She smiled. "I think that's the first time in history that you've ever said that." She accelerated down the road speeding back towards the city. She put on her groughest voice, "Prepare yourself," she growled, "For tonight, we dine, in Manhattan!"

Chapter Seventeen

They arrived in New York City a little after sunfall and parked the beat up old car near the north end of Central Park. As they climbed out of the junk heap, Di took a second to snap off the side and rear view mirrors, handing Marcus the two side mirrors.

"Best you have the heavy artillery." she said. "I have a feeling that only one of us can beat the cockatrice with our eyes closed and it isn't the one of us that needs to." she winked. "Just make sure to point them at the head. It has to see itself to die."

Marcus nodded and clenched his hands tightly around the two mirrors, the fiberglass bending in his hands almost as much as his will did as he realized how crazy this all was but, despite that, he did his best to put on a good bravado.

"Killing a giant dragon chicken, how hard could that be?" he laughed uneasily, pretty sure he knew it was going to be the hardest thing he ever did and most likely the last thing he ever attempted.

"I know right?" Di skipped ahead, he was reminded of the first night that he met her, when she had been so care-free. She had lost a lot of that and had started to put on an edge after George had been murdered. Marcus smiled again, it felt good to have his dragon back.

They walked through the park along Birdie Path for a while and Marcus continued to feel more and more uneasy. As they walked along he did his best to channel and store whatever magic that he could from the plants and trees around him but the fall temperatures had made many of them go dormant, he had gathered up a good bit of power but it felt nothing like what it had when he channeled the shield at the Ranch. This was more like drinking an energy drink when you were already exhausted, like he was moving quickly but he was only seeing half of what was happening around him.

As they rounded the corner at the Charles B. Stover Bench, they saw a glow coming from Belvedere Castle. Di pulled Marcus down into the brush to sneak their way up closer. She motioned for him to stay low and started crouch walking forwards. Marcus followed closely behind as they made their way towards the castle.

When it came into view, they saw a group was

gathered out in front, chanting and playing drums. The crimson robed figures swayed side to side with waist high drums, surrounded by an array of mirrors that encircled the towering building. There were dozens of cultists and hundreds of mirrors.

"So what do you think? Maybe it's a meetup?" Marcus whispered to Di. She gave him a shove and an "Are you kidding me?" look, then smiled, faked mulling it over, and shook her head.

As the cultists kept beating on the drums, the tempo picked up and the volume grew louder and louder, creating a frantic beat that felt more like a shark feeding frenzy than an actual rhythm and, from the outer ring, one figure stepped out, arms outstretched. It threw back its hood, revealing his face. It was Kallis. Marcus moved forward to attack but as he passed Di she grabbed him and pulled him back down, pressing a finger to her lips to silence him.

"Tonight, brothers and sisters, we make our final ascension. We step into the light to bring about a time of darkness, a reign that has been more than ten millenia in the making. Tonight we finally will come out into the world as the supreme beings that the Gods had always intended that we be and the world will know the power that magic holds." He thrust his arms out and the drums stopped.

"I have traveled with many of you for many years and I thank you all for your devotion. Each of you has played a role in this that you could not comprehend. I am thankful for each of you and for the sacrifice that this has been for you. I must now ask, as the Sisters three told me but an hour ago, for one more sacrifice." He raised his arms and athames pulled from half of the cloaks around the circle. The identical silver blades floated level with the ground, their crystal handles casting a prism of light when they caught the light from the torches, creating a circle around the group. "With this sacrifice, we welcome a new era, where magic will go to those who deserve it and where those who use it will rule!" He bellowed and the drums started back up, feverishly playing as a fire burst from the center of the circle at the top of the castle's tower.

The cultists who stood in front of the floating knives put down their drums and stepped forward in unison, impaling themselves on the neck level knives and took a silent step back and falling dead.

"With the blood given freely tonight, by the wishes of my Gods and the power of the universe, I call upon you, the great cockatrice. Come and test me to find me worthy of the final gate." The drums, again, cut off. Nothing happened. Murmuring started in the crowd.

Di leaned over to Marcus and nudged him, "That's my mom for ya." she winked in the darkness and Marcus shuddered. He had just watched no fewer than twenty people kill themselves in the name of their deity all as part of a prank perpetrated by Di's mother. He started to worry about what misinformation they might have been given.

Kallis started up again, "With the blood given freely tonight, by the wishes of my Gods and the power of the universe, I call upon you, the great cockatrice. Come and test me to find me worthy of the final gate." Again nothing. Di snickered a bit too loudly and Kallis turned to their position.

"Who's there?" He shouted. When there was no response, he gestured to the two closest robed people and hissed, "Investigate, kill whatever is there." and they turned and started towards where Di and Marcus hid.

"Wait for it." Di whispered, the cultists were twenty feet away. "Wait for it."

Marcus watched her as she raised both hands out and started channeling the two as they approached. She pulled her hands back quickly and they dropped dead.

"Now!" she yelled and jumped out of the bushes surprising Marcus who had received no indication that this was even remotely the plan. He too ran out of the bushes, following her as he quickly shoved the mirrors, as best he could, into his pockets. On the run, he started channeling the nearest set of robes as he shot as many bolts as he could blindly into the crowd of surprised worshippers, striking a few that were unlucky enough to be standing in the right place, throwing them back through the air. Di was doing the same, just at a much higher speed. Spell after spell flowed out of her, throwing people two at a time against anything hard that she could find. Screams filled the air long with sickening crunches as bodies fell limp against the ground.

Di led the charge into another set of bushes and ducked down. Marcus was immediately behind her.

"A few more like that and we might actually take this as a clean sweep." She was smiling and panting, sweat dripping down her face. Bolts of light and crackling energy shot around them in the bushes, some too close for comfort and they started moving again.

Marcus scanned the lawn to see if he could find Kallis, but he was nowhere to be seen, a trick that Marcus would not fall for again. Without their leader, a few of the cultists panicked and started to run away, only to be struck down by an invisible force, most likely Kallis punishing the deserters.

Di pressed in closer to the group, pulling the life from two more and running straight towards a group of six. From about ten feet away she launched herself into the air like a ninja in the movies and started to rapidly spin, faster and faster until she was a blur in the sky. A purple disk formed under her and she dropped down on them, crushing them flat into the ground in a pile of broken bones and sprawling limbs. Marcus mentally noted that he would have to make time later if he got out of this to get sick from the memory of seeing that and maybe talk to Di about her rage, but for now it was serving their purpose.

From his left, towards the castle, Marcus heard a loud gong and, for a moment, the fighting stopped, everyone turning to see what had caused the sound. He looked over just in time to see Kallis removing the Cockatrice carving from over the door. He raised it over his head and before Di or Marcus could get a spell off to hit him he threw it against the ground. There was a loud roar, like that of a screaming lion, that filled the air and a thick smoke poured into the area around the castle.

The light from spells tunneled through the smoke blindly, casting tall shadows of the people trapped inside of it. Then another shadow appeared, massive crashing sounds filling the air followed by a deafening roar. A massive four legged creature with a head that had the shadow of a sharp edged blob and a massive tail. With another roar there was the sound of shattering glass around them and the smoke started to dissipate. Marcus saw that around him, all of the mirrors had shattered to the ground and in front of him was one of the most horrifying monstrosities that he had ever seen.

The simple chicken dragon that he had seen in his mind's eye had nothing on the twenty foot tall sixty foot long creature that stood in front of him, scales covered its body all the way up to its spine which was filled in with feathers that blended up into two gray black wings that looked like those of a bat. The head of the cockatrice didn't look like that of a rooster, but more like something from one of the altered images in advertisements from PETA talking about the horrible genetic deficiencies that the inbreeding of corporate farms led to. Its head was covered in scales with a few loose feathers along a jaw that led to a beak that opened revealing hundreds of rows of razor sharp teeth. Its eyes glowed with a rusty orange that darted around angrily.

Di grabbed his face and pulled it towards hers, blocking his view "The eyes!" she yelled, "Don't look at the eyes." Marcus immediately looked down at its feet, realizing how close to death he had just been in that moment.

The feet weren't any better, there were four of them, scaly and tipped with five, not three, razor sharp talons that jetted out from toes that moved more like fingers than toes really should.

"Ahh crap." Marcus said. He watched as the cultists turned their attention to it, a few of them casting spells hoping to help in slaying it but every beam and bolt bounced off its scales. It charged them.

With a massive exhale of silvery air, five of them dropped to the ground writhing in agony as their skin boiled and fell off their bodies. It picked up another two with its front claws and smashed them into the ground repeatedly, turning into a mush that seemed inspired by Di's recent display. It then turned to Kallis, who stood on the steps of the castle in wide eyed horror, realizing that he had been lied to by the Sisters.

"I am Kallis," he announced, "Heir to the Throne of Earth and Champion of Chaos. I am here to face the final Ga..."

He was interrupted as the Cockatrice came down on him with its gaping maw and snatched him up like a bird would a lizard. With a few hefts it swallowed him whole.

"Yes!" Marcus yelled, pleased with this end for Kallis. The Cockatrice turned and looked at him and their eyes met. For a moment nothing happened.

It started in his hands and feet, Marcus felt a cool tingling, almost like they had fallen asleep. The tingle grew through his body, rapidly changing from a mild discomfort to the sensation of thousands of ants crawling through his skin wearing salt soaked cleats. He looked down and brought his hands up to his eyes. They started turning gray and, to his silent horror, started to flake away like ash.

"Marcus!" He heard Di yell out to him, but he didn't have enough time to see her as she ran towards him. It took less than a second for his body to blow away, Marcus Grey was dead.

Chapter Eighteen

A bright white light filled Marcus' vision as he opened his eyes. It was exactly what he had always expected. This was his number one end of life scenario. Extending as far as he could see was a floor of fluffy white clouds and sunlight. The pain was gone, the world was gone from around him. He pushed himself up and looked out. As far as the eye could see there was nothing but clouds. He smiled, this wouldn't be a bad place to spend eternity. With a deep breath he took in the sweet smell of cinnamon and, he couldn't be sure but, he was pretty sure that he could smell the beach and sunscreen from his favorite vacation when he had finally scraped up enough money to go somewhere after moving out of his childhood home.

There was a cough from behind him and he turned

around, startled. Behind him sat a row of raised seats, twenty feet tall, each with a person tall enough for their feet to touch the ground sitting in it. Of the eighteen sitting in front of him, he recognized two. One was Demi, who sat there smiling, and next to her, perched on the chair, was Pach. Around them were seven other smiling faces and to the right of them, nine more frowning.

Demi reached out a hand, palm up, to accentuate her declaration, "I welcome you, Marcus, to the afterlife." she winked. "This is the end of your journey. You have done well." her smile glowed a brilliant white.

"But I failed." he said, "Which side wins?"

"Well that's why we are here Marcus, you did fail. Again and again in some brilliant fashions throughout history I might add." Marcus felt a pang of anger that he quickly moved to swallow. "You were however able to outlast the greatest of the champions of the chaos, even if you did not slay him yourself."

A few grumbles erupted from the right side of the group. A man with the body of a human and, from the neck up, the body and head of a snake exposed dripping fangs and hissed, something rattling under his clothes as a purple skinned man with a hammer and wisps of white clouds for hair banged a hammer against the clouds below him a few times, generating sparks that shot out violently, threatening Marcus.

"Now," she said holding up a hand. "We have a decision to make." she placed her hand delicately back into her lap. "We have agreed that the reincarnation cycle ends with you and Kallis, but the agreement had been to find who would win out over the two of you and the results were... unclear." She looked over at the group that Marcus had decided were the bad guys.

"So, what now?" He asked.

"Well, a championship is not worth having if there is not a champion." This statement was met with nods by both sides. "We are sending you back, just one more time, to make it through the last of the champions. If you live we win, if you die, we lose. Plain and simple."

Marcus got angry and didn't bother hiding his distaste for the forced suffering. "And what if I refuse?" He snapped back.

"You don't have a choice, dear. We are sending you back regardless of your wishes" Demi's smile fell. "Do not overestimate your position, you are little more to us than a shell is to the ocean." She raised her hand again, her fingers in a snapping position. "Good luck, Marcus. May you prevail in the light." and she snapped her fingers and the group disappeared. All except for Pach.

The alpaca walked up to him, shrinking in size as it approached. Tied around its neck was a scroll that had "Marcus" written on the outside. He opened it up and read:

Marcus,

I am sorry about the pretense of the Council, we have our ways and, as you can imagine, this was not a choice made lightly. To be honest, we have been cheating more than the light would like to ever admit and certainly more than the dark would presume. But the rules have changed, the Chaos is being allowed to have all of their champions on Earth at once. They will be everywhere. They will be thousands.

We believe in you, but you might want to try something a bit more reliable than mirrors.

Take this.

My eternal love,

Demi

Marcus studied the scroll for a few more read throughs and rolled it back up, looking at Pach for what he was supposed to take, hoping a little in the moment that it would be a sword or some cool staff. He pocketed the scroll and stared at Pach, who stared back, chewing on invisible grass as it watched him, unwavering.

Pach let out a bleat and Marcus felt his body being pulled back together. The world around him started to dim and after a moment he was back in the park, with Di running up to him, the tears on her face turning to a look of confusion.

"What the..." She started.

He looked at her and grinned. "My name is Marcus Grey, and I am ready." he said.

Chapter Nineteen

Marcus laughed and Di ran up and punched him.
Hard.

"You idiot!" She yelled. "What the hell was that?"

"I don't know, the Gods want the games to continue,
at least for another round." He shrugged and felt something
wriggle in his pocket making him jump.

As he grabbed for it, whatever was in his pocket then
bit him with tiny sharp teeth that felt like needles plunging
into his fingertips. He reeled back holding up his finger,
blood already running down it, and, as he did, whatever it
was climbed up his body and under his shirt. After what felt
like more than a minute of wrestling with it, he finally pinned

the furry creature against his chest and pulled it out. A look of disgust crossed Di's face. It was a weasel.

"Where the heck did you get that?" She screamed.

"My pocket apparently, must be a gift from the..." He trailed off as the cockatrice let out a loud crow. He had completely forgotten about the cockatrice. He looked down at the weasel and back at the feet of the monster that had turned its attention to the last two living creatures. Well, the last three. It started barreling down on them and Marcus snapped back to attention, turning and running, weasel in hand, through the field towards the water behind the castle. For some reason, one that had somehow bypassed his New York instincts, he associated the water with safety.

"Gah!" Di huffed behind him, the sound of the feet of the cockatrice barreling down on them, "I get it now!"

"What?" he yelled back over his shoulder, not turning to look back the steps growing louder and his heartbeat louder still.

"Throw it!"

"What?" He yelled again.

"Throw the weasel!"

He raised his arm, weasel in hand, aiming at the lake.

"No, for the love of... Throw it at the cockatrice!"

The last line of the prophetic recitation of the Sister's riddle ran through his mind and he understood. "Pop goes the weasel!" He yelled and turned and threw the weasel at the cockatrice, aiming high above his eyeline. It squeaked, like a dog toy, as it flew through the air, a furry snake tumbling uncontrollably towards an ancient monster, and hit the bounding beast square in the side.

Marcus stopped and watched as the weasel clung to the feathered back of the cockatrice and scurried along, running up its spine. The Cockatrice stopped in its tracks, raising its claws to try and get the little creature off its back.

In a barely noticeable movement, the weasel raised its head and plunged it down, biting into the flesh below it.

The cockatrice reeled back and let out a scream that filled the park. Around where the weasel stood, the skin started to turn to ash and float away, just as Marcus had, a rim of embers expanding across its body, carving holes in its flesh. A few stumbling steps was all that the cockatrice had before its entire body disintegrated into the air. The weasel dropped and Marcus reached out to float it over to him, stopping it from hitting the ground. He set it down softly in front of him and it sat there. Just looking at him expectantly.

"Good job little guy." He smiled and nodded at it. It chittered back like they were about to make conversation and it then ran up his leg and up his body, finding a quick perch on his shoulder and biting at his ear, hard enough that it drew blood.

"Alright piss off!" Marcus said taking a swipe at it only to be met with more angry chittering as it ran to his other shoulder.

Di smiled, "Looks like the Gods gave you a familiar." she laughed, "Dude, a weasel! What a joke, those things reek!"

He frowned at her, "Leave him alone!" He said jokingly, "He's my familiar." Something about saying it out loud made him feel warm. A weasel was better than a staff any day. He had never had a pet and the weasel was as good as any he could think of. He looked down at the weasel and realized he would have to name it and as his mind drifted to domestic thoughts he realized how tired he was.

"So what's next?" He asked Di with a lazy slur.

"What do you mean?" She looked at him quizzically.

"Well isn't there some sort of a gate or hurdle or something? I throw a weasel and I gain the Gods' favor?"

"Well..." she shrugged, "I've never gotten this far before. I mean, it could be."

They looked over to where the cockatrice had fallen and, hovering over the broken shards of the carving that had released it, was a silver orb, electricity crackling over it.

"Then again, maybe that was a bit too hopeful." she sighed, "Ahhh here we go!"

The two of them walked over and got about three feet away from it. Nothing happened. Marcus took a step forward and was met with a blinding light and a shock that ripped through his body. It took a few seconds for him to adjust from the burst and for the black spots that floated in his vision to dissipate and once again he was in a pure white expanse.

He turned and looked for Di, but she was not there. "What am I dead again?" He yelled, actually a little bothered, his voice echoed off invisible walls.

"Good job, Marcus." A booming male voice rang out in a deep southern accent like a hammer made of a fine whiskey. "You have completed your first task... ever."

Marcus didn't know if this voice was specifically talking about his current life or the ones before but he did know that, whoever this was, he was not pleased with the conversation so far and his face likely gave it away because it continued.

"Don't look like that!" It said in a more soothing boom, "This is a time of great revelry, you should feel good about this accomplishment! This is the first time that you have made a single triumph for the forces of good."

Marcus' frown turned to something of a prideful grin that he, embarrassed by it, tried to hide. "So then there is some sort of a gate that I need to make it through?" He asked, trying to push past the fact that he had just killed a mythical beast with a weasel and was likely the first person in history to remember being reincarnated, or brought back to life by gods, or whatever it was that he had just done.

A glowing white gate appeared a few yards ahead of him, outer rim made of a soft purple stone that glowed with a series of blue runes that gave off a calming aura.

"That would be this one right here." Marcus could not see the source of the disembodied voice but he was sure that it was smiling and, for once in weeks, he felt safe in the company of a stranger.

Marcus took a few steps forward to enter the gate but the voice stopped him.

"You are setting out on a journey that you will likely not survive. The friends you hold will keep you safe, don't be a fool and keep your enemies close. Kallis was a minor challenge compared to what you are going to face, a force powered by wrath and hate. The road ahead will be wrought with far worse than you have seen." it warned.

Marcus took a hard breath and nodded and stepped through the threshold of the gate and, once through the light, he was plunged into darkness. Around him stars started to come into focus. The stars grew in size as if they were getting closer until they grew into eyes, thousands of eyes filling the cold darkness, all of them looking at Marcus.

He blinked and they were gone, his mind filled with visions. He saw pyramids and jungles, ziggurats and villages, large sharp teeth and blood. Screams filled his head, the voices of thousands of souls that he had somehow known had been taken by something evil. Then he felt an overwhelming sense of pressure as the eyes returned, nearly blotting out the darkness around him and a light rose, revealing a face that shook him to his core. Thousands of eyes filled a face of something large and covered in red hair. As the light got brighter, Marcus could make out a massive ape creature, it's teeth barred and floating in front of him were nearly quadruple his size. It let out a howl that made the hair stand up on Marcus' neck and he closed his eyes as the hot air blew in his face.

When he opened his eyes back up he was back in the park, the orb still floating and Di standing next to him. The orb slowly lowered and stopped crackling.

"I guess that was it," Di shrugged looking at him. She noticed the look of shock on his face. "What?" she asked, completely unaware that Marcus had been somewhere else for nearly ten minutes.

He did his best to shake off the vision, something about the screech of the creature was still vibrating through his bones, reverberating through his spine. He shuddered, "What do you know about giant monkeys in pyramids?"

She laughed at the question, "What?"

"I just had a vision," he said, explaining everything that he had just seen.

"Well, crap." Di said, "I have no idea what that is." She started walking out of the park, stepping over bodies and burning scorch marks on the ground and Marcus followed. "Sounds like we need some coffee." She shrugged.

"And a burger," he chimed in, jogging along to catch up, the weasel chittering in his ear. He already knew it was going to be a long night.

The trio made their way out of the park in silence, even the weasel picking up on the cue. They made it almost ten feet from the entrance when Marcus' arms shot out to hold back Di. Sitting on a post, at the center of the exit to the park, was a tall black raven. A pang of panic hit Marcus.

"Herschal?" he leaned in as if he were actually going to be able to figure out if this bird was his neighbor's old bird.

A playful male voice from behind them made the weasel shriek in his ear stacattoing the surprise, "Of course you guess that, Marcus? First, try, you always manage to surprise us."

Marcus spun around and found himself face to face with two men and a woman in coordinated green, orange, and blue suits and matching boots. He knew them immediately, even if he had no idea what was going on and had never seen them before. Toko, Renard, and Molly flashed massive grins and struck a pose like carnival performers landing an aerial stunt.

"We didn't think that you would be able to figure it out!" The middle of the trio said, Marcus was pretty sure that the orange suit meant that this was Renard. Renard dove into a deep bow and the other two followed in suit. Marcus came to understand what was happening too slowly, this was their tactic, a distraction. He spun around but Herschal was too fast.

A tall bald black man with lanky proportions loomed over Marcus. Despite being too thin and too tall for natural human proportions, he held himself like a butler who knew too much and couldn't be fired. "Marcus," he said, in the strong voice that Marcus remembered from the Loretz, "Sarge is missing, we need to talk."

Made in the USA
Coppell, TX
25 March 2021